Roberta Latow has been an art dealer with galleries in Springfield, Massachusetts and New York City. She has also been an international interior designer in the USA, Europe, Africa and the Middle East, travelling extensively to acquire arts, artefacts and handicrafts. Her sense of adventure and her experiences on her travels have enriched her writing; her fascination with heroic men and women; how and why they create the lives they do for themselves; the romantic and erotic core within – all these themes are endlessly interesting to her, and form the subjects and backgrounds for her novels.

Praise for Roberta Latow's novels:

'A wonderful storyteller. Her descriptive style is second to none . . . astonishing sexual encounters . . . exotic places, so real you can almost feel the hot sun on your back . . . heroines we all wish we could be . . . irresistible'   *Daily Express*

'The fun of Latow's books is that they are genuinely erotic . . . luxurious . . . full of fantasy. She has a better imagination than most'   *The Sunday Times*

'Passion on a super-Richter scale . . . Roberta Latow's unique brand of erotic writing remains fresh and exciting'   *Daily Telegraph*

'Latow's writing is vibrant and vital. Her descriptions emanate a confidence and boldness that is typical of her characters . . . you can't help but be swept along by them. A pleasure to read'   *Books* magazine

'Sex, culture and exotic locations'   *Guardian*

'Intelligently written . . . definitely recommended' *Today*

Also by Roberta Latow

Embrace Me

Roberta Latow

HEADLINE

First published in 1999
by HEADLINE BOOK PUBLISHING

First published in paperback in 1999
by HEADLINE BOOK PUBLISHING

10 9 8 7 6 5 4 3 2 1

ISBN 0 7472 5957 7

Typeset by
Letterpart Limited, Reigate, Surrey
Printed and bound in Great Britain by
Clays Ltd, St Ives plc

HEADLINE BOOK PUBLISHING
A division of the Hodder Headline Group
338 Euston Road
London NW1 3BH
www.headline.co.uk
www.hodderheadline.com

For Claude Ury
in gratitude for his long, continuing and patient
friendship

A soul that loves you
and a heart that beats to the tune of
memories.
Embrace me.

The Epic of Artimadon

Chapter 1

Nothing remarkable ever happened in Sefton Under Edge until in the early hours of one June morning when a car was found between the Oxfordshire village and a neighbouring stately home, Sefton Park. Abandoned, doors left open, headlamps still on, the BMW was parked across the road, keys still in the ignition.

The village postman, Arthur Harris, stopped his small red van some distance from the offending vehicle. With the motor still running, he contemplated the somewhat sinister sight of the abandoned car by the early morning light filtering through the luscious green leaves of the woods to either side of the narrow private road.

The strangeness of the scene was compounded by the contrast: birds bright with song splitting the luscious silence, mist rising from the woodland floor, dew drops still on the grass. Free-standing, three-storey high stone walls and arches, alone, on a blanket of bright green grass: the ruins of a Tudor stately home on the rise at the end of the road looked all powerful, proud, arrogant against the pearly grey sky.

The postman was surprised to see the obstacle barring

1

his way to Sefton Park, the beginning of his round. It was out of order, an intrusion into a place that reeked of solitude, undisturbed beauty, civilised lives, and it would ruin his schedule. Suddenly he saw the incident as somehow threatening, more serious than a mere car blocking his way.

Arthur had been delivering the post to the village and Sefton Park for so many years he felt protective of the community and the people living in it. He saw himself as a lifeline to the outside world for the villagers and especially the Buchanans, Miss Marguerite Chen who lived in the Dower House, and old Miss Plumm. They were his favourites. Six days a week, he delivered the post and fresh brioches to Sir James and his sisters who lived in the stately home that had been occupied continuously by their family, the Buchanans, for four hundred years. Arthur did odd bits of shopping for old Miss Plumm, as well as deliveries for the village shop, the butcher-cum-fishmonger, and Miss Marble who ran the tea room.

After a moment he cut the motor, and walked briskly to the car. To his initial relief he saw nothing terribly untoward – he tried to ignore the red fingerprints on the window next to the driver's seat. He could not. Back in the van he wondered what to do next. Jethroe Wiley, he decided. Yes, the publican of The Fox would know what to do. He was, after all, a retired policeman.

Arthur sped back to the village, trying to reassure himself there was nothing in the least sinister in his discovery. Just another abandoned vehicle, in fact. He parked the van and started his usual tour around the village, delivering the post and asking at every door whether they knew who owned the abandoned car. No one did.

There was something timeless and romantic about Sefton Under Edge, something fragile and vulnerable. It was a place from another time, maybe even another world. Several large period houses, including a manor house enclosed by high Cotswold stone walls, overlooked a duck pond edged with bullrushes and flag iris. The surrounding woodland was dense with specimen trees: and wild rhododendrons twice the height of a man.

But Arthur could not put out of his mind the discovery of the abandoned car. Thanks to that the stop that should have been his first would now have to be his last, making him late for Sir James and Miss Chen.

He was just about to ring the pub's bell and report his find to Jethroe Wiley when he realised there could be a perfectly simple explanation. The driver was most probably up at the house. Sir James Buchanan and Marguerite Chen, who lived in the Dower House among the ruins, were well known for their policy of keeping open house for friends. Arthur smiled with relief. Yes, that was by far the most likely explanation. No need to go troubling Jethroe Wiley after all.

Arthur's last stop in the village was always at old Miss Plumm's cottage. He walked in, calling out, 'Miss Plumm, it's Arthur. I've brought you the linen you asked for.' In the kitchen he went directly to the kettle and switched it on. He looked around him. Miss Plumm had already laid out two cups and saucers, the tea pot, and a plate of biscuits. The postman and the eighty-two-year-old spinster had been having a morning cup of tea and a gossip for the last twelve years. She was the adored friend of everyone in the village, had lived here all her life and stories about her abounded.

'Good morning, Arthur,' she said, as she entered the kitchen from the garden carrying a basket of freshly cut roses.

'Good morning, Miss Plumm.' The postman was charmed as always by the old lady's beauty and grace, as was everyone who met her. How he would like to have known her when she was in her prime! At her late age she was still a seductive creature.

'I'm running late this morning because a very strange thing has happened. An abandoned car, doors open, the keys still in the ignition, is blocking the Sefton Park road about halfway between the village and the house. I've questioned everyone I can find except Jethroe Wiley and the people at the Park. I wonder if I could borrow your bicycle to get around the car? I really should get up to the big house and see what's going on.'

Miss Plumm seemed to pale slightly at this news, but said nothing. She took a sip from her cup before she told him, 'I don't think you should delay in speaking to Sir James and Marguerite. If they have no idea whose car it is, I think you should call the police. Who knows what happened to the driver? You didn't touch anything, did you?'

He left soon afterwards, placing the post and fresh brioches in the bicycle's reed basket and waving goodbye to Miss Plumm. True, he could have phoned the residents of the Park but he still had his job to do, delivering the mail. Seeing the car a second time a sense of blackness – almost of evil – descended on him again. Cycling as fast as he could to get around the BMW, Arthur didn't even bother to look into the car this time but kept his eyes on the outline of Sefton Park.

The Fox was renowned for its antiquity, its home-brewed beer and real pub food: steak and kidney pudding, Lancashire hot pot, grilled trout, ploughman's lunch, a board of English cheeses, sticky toffee sponge pudding, jam roly-poly.

People from the surrounding villages as well as Sefton Under Edge frequented the pub, a clutch of interesting characters, some of them with famous faces. Jethroe Wiley was a born host. He disliked strangers who behaved intrusively, yuppies and lager-louts, and was clever about deterring undesirables, knowing how to create an atmosphere that drove them away with no desire to return.

Occasionally a tourist strayed from the beaten track to The Fox's front door. Enchanted by their find, the hidden England of their imagination, they spoke in whispers so as not to intrude.

Jethroe received enough custom from the locals and their friends that he could afford to be fussy. The three bedrooms on the first floor were charming and usually rented out to writers who were there to work or friends of the villagers who did not wish to impose as house guests.

Had Arthur rung the bell at The Fox he would not have found the publican in, which would have been the second strange thing he'd encountered that morning because Jethroe never left the pub unattended, and the cleaner and barmaid did not arrive till gone eight. Selina, the cook, and her helper, Chippy, having done the day's shopping arrived anywhere between eight and nine.

As he approached the iron gates before the Park, the postman heard a shot. He braked and nearly fell off Miss Plumm's bike. There was a rustling in the wood nearby; a flurry of barking and growling by at least two dogs. A hunter or a poacher looking for game? His heart racing, Arthur mounted the bicycle and pedalled as fast as he could through the open gates, wondering who could be in the wood at that hour. At this time of year it was rough shooting only, unless Sefton Park was culling? He turned round to look back over his shoulder and recognised Jethroe Wiley's Dalmatians as they burst from the wood on to the road.

A large man appeared from the dense wood behind them. A hunter without a gun? At first glance, Arthur thought it was Jethroe but there was something strange about this man's gait. The red cap was right, and the dogs, but the way he moved was all wrong. Jethroe did not have a limp. Yet another thing out of order this morning. The publican never allowed anyone else to run his dogs for him.

The drive by passed the Tudor ruins and the Dower House, a miniature version of Sefton Park, and carried on up the avenue of ancient limes for nearly three-quarters of a mile to the house itself. By the time Arthur arrived he had convinced himself the right thing for him to do was to put the entire matter into Sir James's competent hands. He himself was, after all, only the postman. What had he to do with such things? He knew for certain now that he was out of his depth and instinct told him the police would have to be called in.

The usual form for delivering the post to Sefton Park was to go up the stone stairs to the front door, enter the house (the door was always left open), placing the post and the brioches on a tray left on the hall table. He only rang the bell when something had to be signed for. Today he rang it anyway and entered the house, placing a parcel and the rest of the post on the table. Sir James appeared from the morning room, dressed in jeans and a fine white linen shirt, a navy blue cashmere pullover draped over his shoulders with the sleeves tied across his chest.

'Morning, Arthur, you're late. Anything wrong?' he asked.

'I didn't hear your van,' quavered Fever, the ancient butler, as he entered the hall from below stairs. The house was notoriously badly run. It was not for lack of trying but more because James and his sisters, Angelica and September, liked living an unstructured life when they were at home. The Buchanans were considered to be somewhat grand gone eccentric or bohemian, depending on who was talking about them.

'I came by bicycle.'

'How odd,' said Fever, and walked off with the brioches.

'That's why I'm late. Well, one of the reasons, Sir James.'

'Is there something wrong?' he asked, realising that the

postman was not at all himself.

'Yes, but I'm not exactly sure . . . I rang the bell because there's an abandoned car on the road between here and the village. It's parked askew, doors open, the headlamps still on, the keys in the ignition. No one in the village knows anything about it and I wondered if you did? Maybe a guest . . .'

'We have none at present. One of our friends might have arrived late, I suppose, and slipped into one of the bedrooms, not wanting to wake everyone. I'll check. You wait here.'

James was halfway up the grand staircase when the postman called after him, 'I'm sorry about this. I should have called the police straight away and been done with it.'

Continuing up the stairs two at a time, James turned to look back and replied, 'No, you were right to come here before calling the police.'

James looked in each of the eleven guest bedrooms, then Angelica's and September's, even though he knew very well there was no one in the house save family. The evening before, he and his sisters, Marguerite Chen and one of her young men, had ridden over the estate by the light of a full moon, had dined on a sumptuous meal then drank, smoked and talked the night away until nearly dawn. Though Angelica and September had slept, James had not. He believed he would surely have heard if someone had entered the house. Yet still he made a pretence of searching for an unexpected guest.

Returning to the postman James told him it was as he'd thought: no one had arrived unexpectedly. He thought it best to go and see if he could recognise the car. Together they walked through several rooms and down the servants' staircase into the kitchen. Only Cook and the cleaners were visible, having breakfast. James greeted them as he and Arthur walked through the kitchen and out into the courtyard where they climbed into a Range Rover.

'Miss Plumm's bicycle . . . I can't leave it here,' said Arthur.

James drove round to the front of the house, flattened the rear seating of the Range Rover and placed the bicycle inside. They took a short cut over the fields, passing through a ruined Tudor gateway as they approached Marguerite's house.

'There is always the possibility the car belongs to one of Miss Chen's friends,' James suggested.

Amazingly they found Marguerite on a ladder dead-heading the climbing old-fashioned white roses that festooned the front of her house. James adored Marguerite for her energy, her lust for life. He wondered how she could possibly be up, never mind working on the roses. He was certain that she had had no more sleep than he, yet only he felt wrecked.

Today her waist-length silken black hair was gathered into a loose braid that reached the small of her back. Her fine pale skin was gently flushed with pink, and her almond eyes were clear and unshadowed. Marguerite had been a feminist celebrity for more than twenty years though, looking at her today, it was hard to believe she had turned forty.

Still on the ladder, she turned and waved as he pulled

up close to the house where from Elizabethan times the Sefton dowagers had lived on the death of their husbands. Until, that is, James had met Marguerite Chen.

Looking as fresh and bright, sexy and charismatic, as she always did, Marguerite climbed down the ladder, saying, 'James, you're the last person I expected to see at this hour. You didn't go to sleep at all! But why am I so surprised? Neither did I. Too much drink and conversation, laughter and – well, you know the rest.'

She kissed him on the lips, lingeringly. She was always reluctant to let him go. Sexual attraction was still strong between them, an impossible kind of love that burned bright and taunted them. Eventually she stepped out of his arms and took her post from Arthur. Marguerite always had a lot of mail. Her arms were soon laden with it: brown manila envelopes bulging with books and manuscripts, letters from all over the world requesting an appearance, an endorsement, an autograph. And fan mail. She received fan mail in every post.

'Good morning, Arthur. How come you have help with your delivery today?'

'Morning, Miss Chen. I'm sorry I'm late only there's an obstruction in the road.'

'An obstruction? That sounds ominous,' she said with an amused smile.

'That's why we're here,' James explained. 'Someone's abandoned a car in the middle of the road. Arthur found it with its doors open, headlamps still on, keys in the ignition. You haven't anyone staying here who might be the owner?'

'No, I haven't. How intriguing.'

She placed the post just inside the front door and announced, 'I'm coming with you.'

Marguerite and James sat in the front of the Range Rover while Arthur shared the back with Miss Plumm's bicycle. They drove from the Dower House through the gates and out of the park. No one spoke. Each of them having private thoughts about the strange happening in their midst. They took some pride in the fact that nothing ever happened in Sefton Under Edge. Would they never again be able to boast that?

James had initially thought that the postman was over-reacting to his discovery of the abandoned car but had been too much of a gentleman to tell him so. He changed his mind about that as soon as the car came into view. What Arthur had not imparted was the sinister aspect of the abandoned car. Something ominous emanated from it and hung like heady perfume in the sweet morning air. James was instantly sure that something dreadful had happened to its driver.

Marguerite broke into his thoughts. 'It's more than someone running out of petrol, James. I don't like the look of this. It gives me the shivers. I'm picking up fear . . . someone in panic . . . running for his life.

'No, two people, a driver and a victim. Why would both doors have been left open if it were only one person?'

They were within fifty feet of the abandoned car when James stopped the Range Rover and cut the motor. The three of them remained silent and made no attempt to leave their vehicle. Finally, James climbed down reluctantly to stand in the road, Arthur following. James

looked across the driver's seat at Marguerite. They gazed
into each other's eyes. There were tears in hers. He
understood her sadness for he too was affected by the
sight. He could think only of fear and flight. Something
vile had happened to the driver of this car. Were they
dead in the wood? Had they screamed to be saved and
no one had heard? And why here? Why deliberately
block the road?

He could understand the tears in Marguerite's eyes,
her fear of what had happened. The whole scene was
redolent of evil. Marguerite wiped her eyes, took a deep
breath and jumped down on to the road. She and James
walked to the front of the Rover. Holding hands, they
walked together to the abandoned car, Arthur several
steps behind them. Neither one of them recognised it.
On looking inside there was the faint scent of expensive
perfume and leather.

None of them touched anything. James wanted to
start the car and park it somewhere else in order to clear
the road but Marguerite stopped him. 'The police will
have to be called to conduct a search of the wood and I
don't think they'd appreciate any interference. The
sooner they tow this away and find the owner, the better
it will be for everyone.'

Marguerite, looking for clues as to why the car should
have been abandoned in such a fashion, discovered
perfectly clear fingerprints of a thumb and forefinger.
They appeared to be sharp, unusually precise and were
red, as if someone had dipped the pads of their finger
and thumb in red ink, which was impossible. Or perhaps
blood. She said nothing of her discovery to James or

Arthur, believing the less said about it the better. This was clearly a police matter.

What she did say as James was calling them on his mobile telephone, was, 'Why here? Why on your road? Did the driver know it? Was he seeking help from you or the girls . . . from me? Oh, damn it to hell! We're for it now. Intrusion, intrusion, intrusion.'

'Not necessarily. They'll tow the car away, ask everyone in the village and us a few questions, search the wood, and if nothing's found it will all be over,' said James.

'I wish I had your optimism. But something tells me you don't believe that any more than I do.' Marguerite had no sooner said it than she realised by the look on James's face that she was right. He too had seen the bloodied fingerprints and preferred not to speak of them.

Standing in the background, Arthur hung his head guiltily, wondering if he was the only one so far to have noticed the bloody prints.

Chapter 2

It seemed to James, Marguerite and the postman, stand-ing close to the abandoned car, that the police were taking an inordinate length of time to answer their call. Quite suddenly James handed the mobile to Arthur. 'It just occurred to me that you're the one who discovered this so you should be the one to report it to the authori-ties. It really has nothing to do with me or my family. It's you they'll want to question.'

He placed the phone in Arthur's hand then moved it to the postman's ear before he had a chance to say anything. Almost at once there was someone on the line and the postman reluctantly reported his find.

'I have to finish my round. After that I can meet you at the station if you want, Jerry?'

Arthur listened to what the local policeman had to say and then told him, 'I'll get someone,' and handed the phone back to James.

'Well, that was lucky, it was my cousin Jerry. He's only a constable but smart as a whip. He should be here in half an hour or less. He says no one should touch the car and he wants someone to stand guard till he gets here. It can't be me, I still have a job to do. People depend on their postman.'

'You carry on, Arthur, I'll get the stable lad to come and stand guard,' offered James.

While Arthur pedalled away to return the bicycle to Miss Plumm, James placed his arm round Marguerite's shoulders and together they walked back to the Range Rover to wait for the stable boy he had called to arrive.

'Do you think someone is lingering in the woods?' she asked.

'No.'

'And you don't think we should speculate further?'

'I think we should put it out of our minds. Come to the house for breakfast. I'm famished and I don't imagine you've had anything to eat this morning?'

'No, not yet.'

While he was calling the cook, Mrs Much, Marguerite studied James. She heard him order breakfast for six to be served at the round table in the oriel window of the great hall.

He usually ordered meals to be served there, when informality was called for, or in the library where a table was placed in front of the fireplace. The morning-room was another favourite place; the landing at the top of the grand staircase yet another. The dining-room, dominated by a cherrywood table that could seat twenty-eight people or when extended forty, was always resplendent with the family silver and reserved for the evening meal, whether it be James dining on his own, with Angelica and September or a group of friends. It was a family tradition that had not been broken in five hundred years.

Whenever she contemplated James, Marguerite could not understand why she could not be faithful to him, why she didn't want him for a husband. She knew he was special: a brilliant mind, a man who wore his heritage quietly and with a style all his own – more casual and bohemian than stuffy and arrogant. His and his sisters' ways seemed to make them more grand, infinitely more remarkable than their peers. James's was a grand life lived casually. She marvelled that he, Angelica and September lived in or used every one of Sefton Park's forty rooms. She adored their flair and panache.

Very nearly every time they were alone together Marguerite wanted James sexually. Her enchantment with their erotic life never wavered. They had come to accept that theirs was sexual love, rich in lust, governed by a genuine deep feeling for each other that would never happen again for them with other partners. A love that lived and flourished in their erotic souls and could go nowhere else. It was an unfettered emotion undisturbed by the outside world, not even the admiration they felt for each other's lifestyle and work.

Jealousy over other lovers was not an issue. If anything, seeing each other with other lovers only excited their passion for each other, fed their lust and triggered their imaginations. The occasional lovers who came between them only made them burn with the heat of renewed desire for each other. They were both content with the erotic life they had together, though this had come sooner to Marguerite than it had to James.

As he put his phone on the seat of the Range Rover, she slipped her arms around his waist and rubbed herself against him, asking huskily, 'We're only four, why did you order for six?'

'Your young lover of last night? The uninvited guest who might appear? You know what our house is like,' he answered.

'Rick's fast asleep and he'll be gone as soon as he wakes.'

James took her roughly in his arms. His passion for her aroused, he kissed her deeply, nibbled hungrily on her lips and then firmly put her from him and stepped away. Marguerite sensed an unease between them that had not existed the night before. She relived for a few minutes the delicious time she had had with her young lover and James.

Marguerite enjoyed young men and changed them often. She was teased about this incessantly by James who claimed she was addicted to young flesh. There was some truth in that but it was more complex than mere youth and sexual stamina – it was pure and delicious sex she craved, with no over or undertones of emotion or love. It was rootless, momentary sensation. Fucking on the wing gave her the most satisfaction. Marguerite enjoyed the hard firm bodies of young men, their lustiness, the careless bravado of their performance.

Last night lust had scented the air. They had wanted the taste and perfume of all things erotic, beautiful people kissing and fondling other beautiful people. Desire mounted in them and they embraced it. James had watched Marguerite and her young lover undress each other as they left the drawing-room for the library. She looked over her shoulder and blew him a kiss. He had smiled, imagining her wallowing in her orgasms, lusting after the young man's throbbing member. He knew how she adored the taste of a man and making love to his sex.

After she had gone James looked around the room. All that was missing was Olivia; his being made love to by her and Marguerite. That had become as much a part of their sex lives as the air they breathed. Passion for their sexuality, their lust, the erotic without boundaries, set them free from the constraints of society. James had wanted Marguerite then and so he joined her and her lover in the library. Once he'd divested himself of his clothes he tapped the young stud on the shoulder and replaced him with his own body, covering the reclining Marguerite. Lust had taken him over then and he took her time and time again until she was lost in a sea of orgasms: hers, her young lover's and James's.

She looked at him now as memories of the night before faded. 'Is something wrong?' she asked.

'Not between us. It's this place. Yesterday it was at peace with the world. Today it makes me uneasy. I want that car gone and to have nothing to do with it.'

Marguerite knew what he meant, but curiosity was drawing her to the abandoned car whereas James was eager to run away from this disruption to their routine lives. That was out of character for him and it surprised her. He was a man who usually wanted to know everything, naturally courageous, able to face anything with good humour and intelligence. He was an explorer who liked to reach into the dark unknown and revel in the bad as well as the good, the ugly as well as the beautiful.

The stable lad arrived and was left to stand guard.

In the car, driving to the house, they said not a word to one another. Gazing at him, Marguerite asked herself, Is it possible he knows more about the car than he's letting on?

On entering Sefton Park Marguerite and James were greeted by the sight of September and Angelica descending the stairs, one behind the other, a large rolled canvas resting on their shoulders. James rushed forward.

'You should have waited for me or called the stables for help,' he chided.

'There really was no need. It's not all that heavy, more awkward to handle,' September told him as Angelica and James placed it carefully on the floor.

'Morning, James, Marguerite. Where have you been at this ungodly hour?' asked Angelica.

'Something dramatic has happened. A car's blocking the road between here and the village, obviously abandoned. You girls wouldn't know anything about it, would you?'

'No,' they answered simultaneously, apparently unmoved by his announcement.

James walked to the hall table, picked up the post and headed for the great hall's oriel window overlooking the gardens. The two-storey high polygonal recess was supported from the ground floor on stone corbels. This and five other such windows in the house still boasted original panes of Jacobean glass. The dining table there was set for six, just as he had requested of Mrs Much. James was followed by his women.

Among his friends and the residents of the village,

when in the company of his sisters and Marguerite, he was always referred to as 'James and his women'. It was always said in good humour and not one of them minded in the least. They all three loved James. For September and Angelica he was very much their world. They were loving siblings, possibly in love. As for Marguerite, she did not in the least mind being labelled one of his women. Because she was. Because she would always be.

September stood behind James's chair and, reaching around him, kissed him on the back of the neck then the top of his head. She took over the sorting of the post, systematically destroying the neatly stacked letters. She grabbed two of them addressed to her and the folded morning paper. James could hardly be angry with her, he'd always indulged September's artistic temperament. He was no different with Angelica. He was inordinately proud of September and respected her paintings, enjoyed her success. He had nothing but love and admiration for Angelica and her first-class brain which had enabled her to become a surgeon. They were girls who worked hard and played even harder, but most importantly they were young beauties who knew their priorities and adored their handsome brother; loved who and what they all were. A family at ease with themselves and the world.

There were crystal goblets of freshly squeezed orange juice at each place setting; a silver salver proffered the brioches. The large round table blazed with colour from a centrepiece of full-blown garden roses. Fever arrived with one of the village girls who carried a heavy Queen

Anne silver tray laden with scrambled eggs surrounded by ribbons of bacon and yet another circle of sausages. Then Mrs Much appeared with another tray containing small fillets of smoked haddock with poached eggs on top. Fever managed to carry a silver basket lined with a fine white linen napkin that covered a small mountain of toast.

The hot dishes were placed on marble-topped consoles mounted on plinths in the form of gilded swans flapping their wings; above them on the dark panelled walls Queen Anne mirrors reflected the light pouring through the window and the comings and goings of the four famished diners filling their plates. All thoughts of the abandoned car were left behind, replaced by laughter. James and his women, a group of beautiful people bursting with love for their privileged life and being together.

Conversation between them dwindled. James was looking through what remained of his post, Marguerite thinking about her lecture tour. Angelica was going for her third helping when September picked up the newspaper she had snatched from James. She unfolded the pages and shook them out. She perused the headlines and let out a fearful scream. Scrambling to her feet and upsetting her coffee cup, she started trembling from head to foot and wailing with despair. She pounded the table with one hand while she kept staring at the front page of the newspaper. The tears came streaming from her eyes.

Marguerite was the first to reach her. James sat as if frozen to his chair, horrified by September's pain and hysteria which he could feel as if they were his own.

Marguerite spun September round to face her. She shook her as hard as she could but to no avail. Finally she slapped the girl hard across the face several times. September took a deep breath, and another, and another. She pressed her hands over her eyes and a few minutes later had control of herself. Marguerite slid her arms around her and said, 'Sorry to have been so harsh.' Angelica stood at her sister's side. She removed the newspaper from September's hand and without looking at it made her sit down. Angelica automatically took her pulse, saying, 'You're hyperventilating. Take deep breaths. You've had a terrible shock but you're going to be fine.'

September wanted to speak but her mouth was bone dry. She reached for her glass of orange juice but could not bring it to her lips, so severe was the trembling of her hand. She tried once more to drink the juice, holding the glass with both hands. Angelica took the glass from her hands and placed it to September's lips. September drank it to the last drop.

'Better?' asked Angelica.

'Much better,' she answered between the occasional sob.

'Now let's see what gave you such a surprise.'

All the colour drained away from her face as Angelica dropped the paper. Her knees buckled. It took all her strength of will to walk to her chair and sit down. James retrieved the newspaper from the floor and put the pages in their right order. He was prepared for the worst and the worst was what he received.

With a stifling sense of rage and despair he read:

Jet Set Murder
Lady Olivia Killer?

The police are mounting a full-scale search
for Lady Olivia Cinders who was chased
from the Mayfair residence of Prince Ali, an
Arab prince found dead just after ten
o'clock last night. The prince's brother
pursued her through the streets of Mayfair,
shouting to passers-by that she was a
murderer. He and a neighbour later confirmed
the identity of the woman. Lady Olivia is
known to have been an intimate friend
of the deceased.

James stared at the half-page photograph of Olivia
standing with the prince, he in polo clothes, she radiant
under a wide-brimmed hat and sleeveless dress. They
were looking lovingly at one another, appeared to be
every inch the darlings of the mega-rich jet set with not
a care in the world. And now this. He looked around
the table at the three pale-faced women and then down
at the photograph of the girl who had been labelled
'the most beautiful in England'. Everyone was fascinated by Olivia, and why not? She had it all: beauty, a
brilliant mind, a wild streak that only added to her
allure, a libido she had never suppressed and which
enabled her to captivate any man, woman or child she
wanted. She was wealthy in her own right with a proud
aristocratic pedigree. The Buchanans had taken her to
their hearts. Theirs was more than friendship, more

than love. Their feelings for Olivia ran deep. She had been in and out of their lives and Sefton Park for as long as any of them could remember.

Nothing was said for several minutes, all of them lost in memories of Olivia. In one way or another they had been, and always would be, in love with her. That was the way of it from the day she'd first entered their lives as a child.

Sir David Buchanan and his wife Molly had been her godparents and Olivia, orphaned when still a young child, was brought up for much of the time with the Buchanans' children. For James, Angelica and September, even now with this horrible scandal laid before them, Olivia was no less a part of their lives, their extended family. Marguerite could almost feel them closing ranks, loyalty rising from the ashes of something terrible to which they would, if not exactly close their eyes, then at least detach themselves.

James cleared his throat several times before he was able to speak. When he did his voice was sad but firm. 'There are very few facts here and a great many assumptions. The investigation has only just begun. We must stand by Olivia, we are all the family she has. Her friends are ours. My guess is they will remain true to her and take a position not unlike our own: one of silence, non co-operation with the media, availability to the police but above all loyalty to her. It's all we can do for her. If we are questioned we must be honest about Olivia but always play down the dark side of her nature. So far as they're concerned, it must be presented as no more than a game she liked to play.'

'But where has she gone? And why did she run away? Has she done it – murdered her lover? She must be out of the country by now. Who did she go to for help? Was she coming here? The abandoned car . . . Had she been driving it? Was she frightened by someone or something or possibly, at the last few minutes coming up the drive, she realised we would be abetting her escape and she could not bring herself to drag us into her scandal,' said Marguerite.

'Marguerite! If we must question and speculate let us all make a pact – never before anyone outside this room,' James commanded.

Marguerite was taken aback. The tone of his voice brooked no denial.

'I think we should drink to that,' suggested Angelica.

'A vow?' said September.

'If you like,' answered James.

'And smash the glasses in the fireplace! You can't be serious?' said Marguerite incredulously.

Her answer was silence. Angelica rose from her chair and walked to a console table where she filled four small long-stemmed crystal glasses with calvados and placed one in front of each person. She took her seat again then raised her glass and said, 'Olivia – wherever you are.' She drained the calvados in one swallow and immediately broke the stem of her glass on the edge of the table. James was next, followed by Marguerite and September.

Afterwards James rose from his chair and left the room. The three women remained at the table. The calvados seemed to have eased the shock they had suffered.

Marguerite adored Olivia but the young woman was not such an integral part of her life as she was of the Buchanans'. Marguerite had seen just how fiercely loyal they intended to be to Olivia. But what if she was a murderer? The question kept repeating itself in her mind. The other three seemed by their words and actions determined not to let that deter them. Could she follow suit?

Not to have drunk that toast would have alienated her from James, September and Angelica and, she had no doubt, their friends and the villagers. Did the taking of a life mean so little to them that they had not even paused to consider the morality of what they were doing?

Marguerite herself had rallied to Olivia not because she was afraid not to but because she remembered her young friend as one whose passions were many and whose courage to live them to the full, with dignity and joy in life, was uplifting and inspiring. Could a woman like that be a cold-blooded killer? Marguerite could face the truth: everyone is capable of killing if circumstances demand it. And Olivia had run away, an indication she might be implicated. Marguerite knew that the murdered prince and Olivia's dash for freedom would dwell on her mind, whereas the Buchanans would simply ignore any fact that implied her guilt. And that really troubled Marguerite.

Her thoughts were interrupted by James's return to the dining-room. He held in his hands an ebony box inlaid with silver and ivory roses. He told the women at the table, 'Pass the broken glasses down to me. We'll put them in this casket and have them mended when Olivia has come home to Sefton.'

September, recovered now from the shocking news, spoke up. 'Olivia cherished life. She lived for the moment and taught us to do the same. We've all benefited from her generosity and kindness, her endless *joie de vivre*. That's why we all love her – why her beauty of body and soul enslaves everyone who meets her. She is dangerously beautiful and I for one will do anything I can to support and stand by her. I don't believe she has a friend who will not feel as I do.' With that she rose from the table and walked away.

'What we must never forget is that the prince was a most charming cad all the time, a sadist some of the time, a sensualist who had dragged Olivia down into his depraved world where she wallowed in sensation. She assured herself and her friends that she would pull out of that life when she was bored with it. Olivia was strong-willed. She believed, and made us believe, what she said. And now this! To hell with the prince, I say. She loved him and he used her.' Angelica too rose and walked away.

Chapter 3

Gerry and Cimmy Havelock were having breakfast in the garden when he shook the paper open and saw Olivia staring out at him. The *Guardian*'s photograph of her was enchanting: a laughing beauty with her head thrown back and arms open in come hither fashion. He imagined he could hear her laughing.

Gerry read the article and immediately declared, 'Impossible!' He rose from his chair and dropped the newspaper into his wife's lap. Kissing her on the cheek, he told her, 'Don't hold dinner for me, I'll be late.' And was gone before she could say a word.

Fortunately his car was already outside on the gravel sweep. Gerry slipped into the driver's seat and drove slowly away from the manor house. The head gardener, Pringle, was just opening the iron gates. Gerry waved and gave one of his most charming smiles as he drove through them. Pringle raised his cap and called after him, 'Morning, sir.'

'Morning, Pringle. Can't stop, running late.'

Pringle looked at his watch and wondered what the man was going on about. He was spot on time. Gerry

Havelock was habitually punctual. In the twenty years the Havelocks had lived in Sefton Under Edge, Pringle had never known Mr Havelock be late leaving the house.

Cimmy Havelock picked up the paper and began reading about Olivia. Her first thought was of Raife, her son. How he had loved Olivia! Believed she loved him in return. And for a short time Olivia had loved the Havelocks, become a part of their life.

The thing about Olivia was that once you had a taste of her, you always wanted more, much more. She was everything that was lacking in one's own life. Why had Cimmy not realised that before it was too late? Before Olivia, Gerry and Raife had betrayed her with lies and evasions, while ostensibly trying to spare her the pain of their deceit. She had loved Gerry and Raife before Olivia took them away from her, but it had been a blind, unquestioning love. She loved them still but was not so foolish now. And what of her own love for Olivia? Crushed and kicked aside, not by herself but the men in her life, her husband and her son. All had been forgiven years ago but not forgotten by her. No one ever spoke about what had happened. Time had healed the wounds Olivia had dealt them. For several years now, when Cimmy and Gerry's paths had crossed Olivia's, it was as if the entire affair had never happened.

Genuinely sweet of character, submissive, charming in an old-fashioned way, Cimmy was the best of wives to her husband and mothers to her son. She worked for the needy and opened her seven-acre garden, which the eighty-one-year-old Pringle had been working on for fifty-five years, to the public in aid of charity once a year. Yet she screwed up the newspaper and threw it violently in the rubbish bin.

The Reverend Edward Hardcastle did not hear about Olivia by reading the morning newspaper. He received the news from the butcher, Mr Evans, who remarked, 'That lovely, sweet, pretty girl . . . known her all her life, Vicar. Lies, all lies. She's no more done that foreigner in than I have.' And handed the vicar his own copy of the *Mirror*.

The vicar was distressed by what he read. Mr Evans was correct, of course. Olivia – or the Olivia he knew – would be incapable of such an act. He took his packet of bacon from the butcher and headed back to the vicarage. All the way home he thought about Olivia, now on the run from the police. He kept remembering the agony and ecstasy of his suppressed lust for her. How difficult it had been to force her out of his life though finally loyalty to God had triumphed.

Lilith Hardcastle had never guessed the sexual fantasies her husband had wrestled with and finally managed to dispel from his mind. How appalled she would have been to learn that Edward, the man she believed she knew to the marrow of his bones, lusted after a young woman. The Hardcastles were pillars of wisdom and kindness to the village, working night and day for their parish. Their six children, now grown and all at university, when at home filled the vicarage with gaiety and friends. The Reverend Hardcastle and his family exuded an aura of stability, love, contentment. Everyone wanted to be included in their magic circle. Even, for a time, Olivia.

In The Fox for a drink before or after dinner, depending on his workload, Edward would change his collar for the philosopher's hat and join some of the regulars holding forth on how to solve the problems of the world. At a round table close to the bar would be seated the vicar and possibly Lilith, Gerry Havelock, Miss Marble from the tea room, who never said a word from the time she greeted everyone to the time she wandered off home pleasantly tipsy, the retired General and the retired Admiral, who never agreed on anything.

At home, Edward went directly to the kitchen where he knew he would find his wife. He told Lilith about Lady Olivia Cinders as he handed her the bacon. She, like everyone else who heard the news, was shocked. She took a seat at the kitchen table and poured her husband a mug of coffee. Lilith's first words were, 'I don't believe she could do such a thing! We must support her, do something about these accusations.'

'I don't think you should make a cause out of this, my dear,' warned Edward.

'Surely you could give her a character reference?' insisted his wife.

'Let's wait for the right time. If and when we're needed, Olivia knows we will help her. But until she asks for us we'd best stay out of this,' he insisted.

Lilith rose from her chair and went to the cooker. She carried on making breakfast while keeping Olivia in the forefront of her mind. Edward must help! She could not understand his hesitation. It was very unlike him to hold back on anything when he could be of service.

The smell of bacon and eggs filled the kitchen, and

even that incited further memories of Olivia. 'Remember how she loved my fried eggs, Edward? I would make them for her and Beth the morning after one of their sleepovers. Let's pray she's not out there somewhere in the world alone and without friends. Edward, you must try and reach her to let her know she can count on our friendship. Beth will be so upset when she hears the news. After the Buchanans, she was Olivia's best friend.'

'Lilith, Olivia drifted away from Beth and our other children a very long time ago. Let's just wait and see what's really happened before you start a support group for her. What we should do is pray that she comes to her senses and returns, goes to the authorities and clears her name. It would be best for her and for everyone. This village is a haven of peace and love, a paradise to live in. I shudder to think what would happen to it if the police appear here and throw us to the media.'

'Well, you and your cronies at the pub will have plenty to talk about tonight,' was his wife's only reply.

Edward forked into his mouth a piece of bacon and egg, its rich yellow yolk dripping off the silver prongs on to his plate.

'There goes Miss Plumm, off to the butcher on her bicycle, and here comes Jethroe with his dogs, swinging a brace of rabbits.'

Jethroe entered through the kitchen door without even knocking and slammed the rabbits down on the work-top. 'Morning. Thought you might like these for a stew, or marinated in herbs and olive oil and thrown on your barbecue. God, that bacon smells great. Makes the mouth water.'

Lilith placed four more rashers in the frying pan and turned up the gas. 'You will stay for breakfast, Jethroe?'

'Well, since you ask,' he replied with a smile.

Both Edward and Lilith found his appearance in their kitchen, bearing a gift of game, strange to say the least. He behaved as if this was the norm when indeed it was not. Though Jethroe had been in their house innumerable times it had always been by invitation.

As a publican he was first class; as a man a devout sinner and a mean drunk, a notorious womaniser, and not a very discreet one. He treated his current lover Hannah Brite, the barmaid at The Fox, abominably. The occasional bruise on her forearm and face were all too obvious.

'Nice of you to bring us the rabbits, Jethroe. Aren't they wanted in The Fox's kitchen?' asked Edward.

'I got lucky, shot more than we need. I suppose you've heard about the abandoned car and now all the scandal over Olivia? I called my old station in London to get the inside information. It seems she did kill him and got away. They'll catch her in the end. Interpol's already on it. The pub's sure to be full tonight with all this to chew on.'

'I hope you said nothing that will bring them down around our ears?'

'I said nothing, and suggest you do the same when or if she's not found and New Scotland Yard starts digging deeper into her life. Might I suggest you write down where you and your wife were last night. It's conceivable that you might have forgotten by the time the police become aware of who her real friends are. She has many here in the village as well as at Sefton Park. They're bound to come asking for information.'

After Jethroe finished his breakfast he thanked Lilith and left rather abruptly.

'That's the first time Jethroe's ever behaved like that with us – as if he were our bosom friend. Walking in without even a knock at the door, and bringing the rabbits. He's never given us any before! They were just an excuse to pay us a visit, and I don't believe for a minute that it was to warn us to have an alibi ready for last night. Such melodrama,' said Lilith.

'It was more as if he was establishing one for himself – being out shooting last night – and this is the evidence, fresh-killed rabbit,' said Edward as he raised a poor dead beast then laid it neatly on the draining board.

Jethroe had been right about one thing. That evening and well into the night The Fox was as crowded as it could possibly be. The talk was all of the abandoned car, the police roaming through the wood questioning the villagers, and finally of Lady Olivia. The majority of the drinkers agreed it had to be a mistake. She wasn't the sort to be a murderess.

Detective Chief Inspector Harry Graves-Jones was sitting at his desk in New Scotland Yard with a bad feeling about the case to which he had just been assigned. On the one hand he was delighted to be offered such a high-profile murder investigation. On the other, the case had all the ingredients to intrigue the general public: a foreign prince, a beautiful aristocrat who had fled the scene of the crime, high society, mega wealth, glamorous living and playing, sex and politics. The media would gobble up every detail and keep him under constant scrutiny. 'How those bastards on Fleet Street will love this!' he said aloud.

The commissioner, sitting in a swivel chair looking out of the window, spun round to face him.

'Sorry, sir, thinking aloud. Fleet Street . . . the tabloids . . . they'll milk this story dry.'

The commissioner had been droning on about procedure, how the Yard must come out of this one as having behaved impeccably in everything they did to apprehend Lady Olivia. The investigation was going to be doubly difficult because a prince from one of the Gulf States was involved. That meant interference from a foreign government who would certainly put pressure on the Home Office who in turn would pester the commissioner. Harry had only been listening to him with half an ear. The commissioner, as he always did, assumed they would succeed in finding their quarry and delivering her to the courts. For him it was just a matter of days, a week at the most, before they captured Lady Olivia.

The commissioner had followed Harry to his office from the ward room where he had been instructing his officers, thirty-seven of them, to call at every house in Mayfair, question every resident in the hope of obtaining some clues.

'In an investigation such as this one time is your enemy, Harry. At the moment it's on our side. She can't have gone too far. You checked out the London stations and airports, didn't you?'

'There's been no sighting of her. Nothing. But a

woman like that has to have friends. She could be hiding out right under our noses, or they could have driven, sailed or flown her out of the country by now.'

All the while Harry and his superior were talking, Harry kept his gaze on a silver-framed photo of Olivia standing on his desk. She was incredibly beautiful, like fire and ice. She had a classical aristocratic English beauty with a seductive flame that burned bright beneath. He had taken the photograph from on top of the piano in Olivia's drawing-room at Albany on Piccadilly, one of the smartest, most exclusive addresses in London.

'Sir, we're dealing here with anything but a common criminal,' Harry observed. 'It's the privileged classes we'll be dealing with and my guess is they'll close ranks. Lady Olivia's friends and relations and the anglophile Arabs who surrounded the prince will be more of a hindrance than a help. We'll be out on our own on this one. Co-operation will hardly be the name of the game.'

'That's why you were assigned this investigation. You know how to deal with that sort. You can be unorthodox but you never overstep the mark. Run this case any way you like, I'll give you as much assistance as I can and fend off the press as much as is possible.'

With that the commissioner rose from his chair as did Harry. The two men shook hands and the commissioner left the room. Harry sat down again. He took the silver-framed photograph in his hands and studied Olivia's face for a considerable time. He drew her into his subconscious, wanting to carry her with him. He hoped to achieve a sense of her, to get into her head, think the way she would be thinking, predict how she would react to being on the run, so that he could pre-empt her movements and track her down.

Within hours the crazies as well as the Good Samaritans would be calling in with sightings of Lady Olivia. Every last one of them would have to be followed up. If only one per cent of the calls was genuine luck was on Harry's side. He rang the ward room and asked for two young detectives, Joe Sixsmith and Jenny Sullivan.

They entered the room together. The three of them had worked well as a team before. Sixsmith and Sullivan were familiar with this new breed of detective of which Harry was the best New Scotland Yard had to offer. They were somewhat in awe of his crack investigative mind, his posh voice and knowledge of the English aristocracy and how it worked. Behind his back fellow officers referred to him as The Gent, because of his public school and Cambridge education, his Savile Row suits: hound's-tooth, grey flannel; blue fine cotton shirts; the subtle burgundy silk tie, and always the tiny white orchid in his lapel.

Computer literate, he was able to use that together with his agile, enquiring mind and impressive range of contacts. Sixsmith and Sullivan had never met anyone quite like Harry Graves-Jones and they used him as an inspiration to rise that little bit higher in their work. They respected him as a man and loved him as a master detective.

'Anything I should know?' he asked his assistants now.

'No further developments,' said Joe Sixsmith.

'Jenny, I want more men on the house to house.

Extend the search to Knightsbridge, Belgravia and Chelsea now. If our lady's still in London she'll have sought refuge in one of those areas. A hundred men on the streets – see to it. Each hour that goes by is to her advantage. Any sightings, I want to know about them immediately. I'm going to lunch at my club – Joe, you can drive me.

'Jenny, I want you to try the Bond Street shops. Enquire about her and anyone who habitually accompanied her. Find out who her friends are, anything they might know about her. Joe, you can try the restaurants she'd have frequented. Here's a list. Start with San Lorenzo and Harry's Bar.'

Harry's club was Brooks, which had been his father's, his grandfather's and great-grandfather's. A bequest from his Uncle Raymond took care of any bills run up there and the annual membership for Harry's lifetime. Upon Harry's death, the bequest was to pass to his sons if there were any. Uncle Raymond had been Harry's father's brother, a bachelor who'd loved his freedom and detested the very idea of marriage. He'd been reclusive yet strangely social when it suited him, a well-respected High Court judge. Uncle Raymond had adored his nephew and had been a second father to Harry whose own had been as generous as he could afford to be but indifferent as a parent. They had always had a slightly formal relationship. His mother had died soon after Harry had been born. She had been the great love of his father's life, and with her death love and emotion were buried in the same grave.

Another bequest Uncle Raymond had left Harry was

a set of rooms at Albany, a large and elegant Edwardian building set back off the street by iron gates, with a circular drive before the front doors where an impeccably uniformed doorman presided. Albany was famed for its A-list residents. When Harry learned that Olivia Cinders had also lived there he was not encouraged. He had had no intimation of it before the case broke as this was a building famed for privacy, the discreet behaviour of its tenants and the silence of its staff.

On enquiring all he gained, besides entrance to her set of rooms, was the information that she'd rarely used them. That she was more apt to spend a few hours there during the daytime, and was never there at the weekend. That she was adored by the staff, who said they knew nothing about her life except what they read in the papers and did not believe for a minute that she was capable of killing anyone. Harry had known the doormen most of his life. They knew all the liaisons that took place in Albany, and would keep strict silence. Scandal was not Albany's style. Harry knew he had already gathered as much as he was going to from the staff and the board that ran the building. He'd been clever enough not to be so intrusive as to annoy them but knew he'd get no further.

At Brooks he dined alone, watching and listening to the club members. One of their own in such a scandal was bad publicity for the upper classes. It was sure to be a topic of general conversation for at least a few minutes. Harry was just attacking his jam roly-poly when he received his first piece of concrete information.

'A lovely girl, damned attractive,' he overheard. 'The

Buchanans of Sefton Park were inseparable with her; the girls especially will be shattered by any scandal. If Olivia made it to them, she'll be all right, they'll take care of her. She's always run with the best and they won't let a star like her down, no matter what she did or didn't do. It was foolish of her to run away, though. Should have stood her ground no matter what had happened to the prince. A bit cowardly that. The running away, I mean.'

'Do you think she did it, Archie?'

'Early days, Bumpy. If she did it will have been self-defence, of course. A sordid affair, though, whichever way you look at it.'

Harry finished his pudding and took his coffee in the main room. He drank it slowly with beautiful Lady Olivia in the forefront of his mind, afterwards feeling compelled to return to her rooms at Albany.

Chapter 4

It had been easy to trace the owner of the car found abandoned in Sefton Under Edge. The vehicle was London-registered to a Mrs Caroline Wasborough of 28 Hay's Mews, Mayfair. When an officer from the Oxford police department called to verify ownership of the car she claimed she had not even known it was missing. When told by the officer the circumstances in which her car had been found, Mrs Wasborough professed disbelief.

All arrogant, cool detachment she asked, 'Are you telling me that my car has been involved in a crime? What a nuisance! I do hope it's drivable and you can get it back to me some time today?'

'I don't know about that, ma'am. I shouldn't think so. I'd have to ask my chief.'

'Well, put me through to him then,' she demanded.

Chief Inspector Fred Pike took the call and asked far more questions than Mrs Wasborough felt was necessary. She considered his behaviour intrusive and told him so in no uncertain terms.

'My husband will be home at four. I suggest you deal

43

with him if you have anything more to ask. This is too inconvenient! Just get that bloody car back to me *today*!' And she slammed down the telephone.

'Snotty upper-class bitch!' was Fred Pike's verdict.

Forensic had not as yet even arrived in Sefton Under Edge where they would go over the car then have it towed to the police garage in Oxford for a further once-over. Fred Pike smiled to himself because he knew Mrs Wasborough would not have her car back for a very long time if they found anything untoward. When he thought how angry that would make her, he was delighted.

The Chief Inspector's first sight of the car confirmed his gut instinct that this case was trouble. He radioed in to his office and summoned twenty men at once to comb the wood. Forensic arrived while he was still on the telephone. If the search of the woods revealed nothing untoward, nor the questioning of the villagers and the Buchanans, he would put it down as just another stolen car snatched by joyriders.

Several days passed and Forensic had done its work which included analysis of the bloody fingerprints on the window. It was a woman's thumb and forefinger, type B. As a matter of course they ran the prints through the system to see if they belonged to any known criminal and came up with nothing. A search of the woods and interviews of the residents in the area revealed nothing that might help to find the culprits who had stolen the car. Several days had passed. The Chief Inspector pulled all his men off the case but left the file open.

Fred Pike was a good detective, and instinct told him that there was more, much more, to this abandoned car than stealing for a joyride and somehow the Wasboroughs were more involved than they appeared to be. Fred Pike daily expected a call from either Mr or Mrs Wasborough, demanding their car. He found it strange that after his one conversation with Mrs Wasborough, he never heard from them again.

At odd moments through the day Pike would be reminded of that conversation. It still niggled him that she should have been so deliberately rude to him, that she should not have been at all interested in the fact of her car's being stolen, all she had wanted was to have it returned. It suddenly occurred to Fred that Mrs Wasborough was for some reason acting out a role. She had been deliberately rude to him for a reason.

The newspapers, radio and TV were full of the search for Lady Olivia Cinders who seemed to have vanished off the face of the earth. It was all the talk everywhere. Had she committed suicide? Had she got away abroad? The tabloids were dredging up every scrap of smut they could find about Lady Olivia and her prince.

Fred Pike had the habit of breakfasting at a small cafe a few streets from his office. It was the best fry-up for the money that could be found in Oxford. Sally Ann's Cafe was frequented by many officers from Pike's division. He preferred breakfast with them to the chaos of the first meal of the day with his wife and four children whom he adored, but not first thing in the morning.

He, like every officer in the country, was following the Cinders case with a professional eye. Every one of them had their own theory about what had happened on the night of the murder; whether she'd done it or she hadn't.

Where she might be in hiding. Whether she was dead or alive. Talk of Olivia Cinders was all around him while he devoured his breakfast. Waiting for his second cup of coffee, Fred Pike shook out his rolled up newspaper. There was yet another photograph of Lady Olivia. In this one, taken at Royal Ascot, she was flanked to one side by Caroline Wasborough, to the other by her husband Giles. The dead prince was standing at the end, or so the caption told him.

'Holy shit!' exclaimed Fred Pike.

'What's up, sir?' asked one of his men.

'Nothing much. Except we've had the hottest clue to the Cinders case sitting right in front of us for several days and never even saw it! Let's go. Got to get this worked out before I call New Scotland Yard and this Graves-Jones who's running this case. Lucky bastard.'

Harry Graves-Jones was too baby-faced to take seriously, too handsome, too well-dressed and too eccentric. Far too affable to be a detective chief inspector and wield authority. Or so the uninitiated believed. Harry used his looks and manner, his public school and Cambridge education, to catch people off guard. 'Harry Graves-Jones always gets his man' was what they said about him at New Scotland Yard. And he did.

Harry greeted the plain-clothes man on duty at Lady Olivia's front door. The officer let Harry in to her rooms after he'd told his superior that there was nothing to report. It had become a habit, Harry visiting Olivia's rooms before he retired to his own on the floor above at the opposite end of the building. There was a marked difference between the two apartments.

He walked through Olivia's drawing-room, switching on lamps, imagining that that was what she would have been doing on returning home. The room instantly sprang to life. It was her drawing-room, it could not have been anyone else's. Painted a creamy white, the large double cube room, with marble columns and a high ceiling, was furnished in sumptuous fabrics: damasks and brocades, leather and suede, all in many shades of white. There was a concert grand: a white Bechstein. The only touches of colour in the room came from the oriental carpets on the polished wood floors and the painting on the wall: a massive Poussin. The tables were of ivory, as was the odd occasional chair. On every surface stood a seemingly endless collection of silver-framed photo-graphs and several black and white portraits by world-famous photographers: Eve Arnold, Terry O'Neill, Norman Parkinson, Bailey, Donovan.

He preferred the Terry O'Neill portraits which cap-tured Olivia's sensuality. She seemed to shimmer. The photographer had managed to grasp her vitality, her hunger for life in all its many forms. She was an enchant-ress in the same way as Princess Grace of Monaco had been. Her cool, blonde beauty did it all for her.

After interviewing several of Olivia's friends Harry knew he had a fight on his hands. Word was out among the upper echelons of English high society: 'Close ranks.' He rather admired them for their code of honour – 'We take care of our own' – even when it hindered his work.

There was a faint scent of lily of the valley in the rooms. He walked through them all, as he did every evening. And as always he discovered something new about his quarry that served to render him even more infatuated with her, made him understand why she had run away. He had no doubt that she had killed the prince; felt that it had been a murder born of passion, of both love and hate, not coldly premeditated. That she must have been driven over the edge by the intensity of erotic love gone wrong. The clues were all there at the scene. The prince had still been tied to the headboard of his bed, a blindfold over his eyes, a long silken cord round his neck. Mere sexual games. But not so the chiffon scarf stuffed in his mouth nor the dagger that had slit his wrists.

Harry was not releasing these facts or any others pertaining to the sex life of the prince which he had learned from the prince's brother. He had also grasped that Lady Olivia Cinders was driven by a passion for all things sexual and lived her erotic life openly, indulging in it as if it were a toy or a delightful game.

Harry sat on the end of her bed. How he would like to meet a woman such as Olivia! One with the courage of her sexual convictions. He was convinced she had not run away because she had murdered her prince but because she could not and would not face the scandal of her sex life being made public knowledge. It was not in her to see her other lovers' private lives dragged through the press, innocent people being exposed for their dalliance with her.

For all the interviews he and his force had conducted there had not been a bad word said about Lady Olivia. It seemed her kindness and joie de vivre had always been uplifting. Everyone either loved her or wanted to love her. And he could understand that since he had become infatuated with her himself, this woman he had not even seen in the flesh.

After turning off the lights Harry stood for several minutes in the dark. He thought about a ravishing young woman living in such a setting with a three-million-pound family painting hanging on the wall. That life was now in shreds, Olivia a murderess on the run whom he must hunt down. Where could she go? And how would she manage for money? All her bank accounts were frozen while every country in the world was looking to arrest her. Two weeks and still no sign of her, no real clues to go on. Harry knew he had to consider that she might no longer be alive. He could hardly bear to think about that. Olivia was not one to take her own life. If she had been she would not have run away. To be free was everything to her.

When Harry entered his own set of rooms and switched on the lights, he was struck by the differences between them and Olivia's. He had never touched them, had moved into the rooms just as his Uncle Raymond had left them. From childhood he had adored his uncle's set at Albany. Every time he entered them now he never ceased to be amazed that they belonged to him; that Uncle Raymond had left them and their contents to him.

The contrast between Olivia's rooms and his was marked. Harry's were choc-a-bloc with treasures from his uncle's lifetime of travelling: Egyptian artefacts, mostly sculptures, Greek bronzes and black and terra-cotta vases decorated with Minotaurs and young boys trying to wrestle the beast to the ground, Roman amphoras, a collection of Roman glass iridescent with age, a library of rare books, oriental carpets on the floors, Edwardian leather sofas soft and mottled from wear. Eighteenth-century mahogany reading tables and the massive head of a Greek kouros. Draperies of cream silk moray embroidered in tiny silk flowers, festooned and with giant tassels, that had once been in Marie-Antoinette's sitting-room at Versailles, hung in ribbons where the sunshine of centuries had scorched the folds. The bedroom looked much the same, offering a handsome four-poster bed draped in faded yellow silk damask.

Harry enjoyed his home enormously, had spent much of his youth here visiting his uncle. Harry was no cook and dined out mostly or invited one of his lady friends to come and cook him a meal. Otherwise he sent out for Chinese takeaway, his favourite food.

The aroma of roasting lamb and the sounds of Pink Floyd were apparent from the kitchen. He stripped off his clothes and dropped them on the floor as he went through to the small room. Naked, he walked as silently as possible up to Sambella and wrapped himself around her.

She was only one of the many women Harry had in his life. Nineteen years old and a stunning long-legged beauty, she was one of the top mannequins on the Paris runways. The fashion world adored her for her ebony skin, her long slender body, legs that seemed to go on forever, almond-shaped eyes, high cheek bones, and magnificent symmetrical features.

Harry rarely saw her because she was based in Paris and travelled the world for her work. When in London she always stayed with him. They were good friends and magnificent lovers, who knew there was no future for them, only now. He was too old for her but he had been her first sexual partner and periodically she returned to him.

She slipped around in his arms to face him and they kissed. He picked her up and carried her to the bedroom. She wore a transparent white shift and as he placed her on the floor he slid it up over her head. She began to say something. Harry silenced her with another kiss, then told her, 'Shush! Not a word. Sex first.'

Sambella smiled and, taking him by the hand, led him to the bed. Before they lay down together she ran her hands over his body, kissed his chest, sucked on his nipples. With her hands locked around his neck, she raised herself, crawled up his body and impaled herself upon him in one swift, deep thrust. She called out in intense pleasure. With her hands on his hips, legs twined round his waist, she raised and lowered herself on his ample erection. Slowly, deliberately, they fucked for their greatest pleasure. Olivia and everything but sexual ecstasy was forgotten.

When Harry awoke in the morning she was gone. All that remained of her was her scent, jasmine and lemon, a note and her key to his rooms on the pillow. He read it and smiled. A farewell fuck, the best way she knew to say goodbye. It had been a memorable night of lust, a marvellous ending. He smiled, feeling a sense of love and admiration for the young and astonishingly beautiful girl who, it seemed, had now fallen deeply in love with a Sudanese diplomat.

He walked through the rooms looking for a trace of her but she had left nothing, not even the dirty dishes from the night before. Only the scent of her lingered, that and a sense of gratitude that he had had her and they had been so good together. The piercing ring of the telephone broke his moment of sentimentality and Sambella was gone from his mind.

'Chief, I think we've got a break at last. A call from a Chief Inspector in Oxford. He's been working on an abandoned car and thinks there might be a connection between it and the Cinders case,' said an excited Sixsmith.

'Give me twenty minutes and pick me up at the Vigo Street entrance.'

The telephone rang for a very long time before Caroline Wasborough answered it. 'May I speak to Mr or Mrs Wasborough?' asked Harry.

'Mrs Wasborough speaking,' she replied.

'This is Detective Chief Inspector Graves-Jones, Mrs Wasborough. I believe you have had an automobile stolen? I would be grateful if you could give me a time today that is convenient to you so that I might come and discuss the theft with you.'

'Three o'clock, will that do?'

'Thank you, that will do nicely.'

Harry put down the telephone and looked up at Jenny Sullivan and Sixsmith. 'Mrs Wasborough wasn't rude, quite the opposite in fact, and sounded not at all the snotty bitch Chief Inspector Pike said she was. I've made an appointment with her for three this afternoon. I want you both with me and the file on the stolen vehicle which is being faxed to us from Oxford. As soon as it arrives make three photocopies. Bring one to me. I want both of you to study it, have it down pat in your mind. Before our meeting I want to hear anything you have to say about it that might be relevant to our case.'

Harry swivelled his chair around and looked out of the window. He thought about Caroline Wasborough. Instinct told him that she had been waiting for a call from New Scotland Yard. It was the softness in her voice, a sense of resignation and something akin to relief that the call had at last arrived.

Harry and his assistants arrived at the Wasboroughs' mews house several minutes after three o'clock. The door was opened by a white-jacketed houseman. They stepped into an atrium with a fountain and massively tall papyrus growing under a glass roof. It was then that Harry realised the Wasboroughs' London residence was not just a mews house but four mews houses made into one.

The three of them were led through the atrium and into a large, elegant, comfortable-looking drawing-room where they met Mr and Mrs Wasborough and their solicitor, Sir Alfred Menard.

Caroline Wasborough was dressed in a pair of cream wide-legged trousers and a silk blouse with graceful dropped shoulders and balloon sleeves. She had not the beauty or the youth of Olivia but could still be classed as an attractive woman. When she rose from a deep lounge chair four King Charles spaniels, tails wagging and floppy ears dancing, whirled around her ankles and one leaped into her unsuspecting arms. She caught it and laughingly introduced herself and the others in the room, including the dogs.

Sixsmith and Sullivan looked flummoxed. This was clearly not what they'd been expecting. They'd assumed that Mrs Wasborough was going to be defensive and nervous. She was, after all, obviously guilty of aiding and abetting a murderess. Or so they'd assumed by putting the Oxford facts together. It was almost as if Caroline Wasborough understood their disappointment because, after introductions were made, she suggested, 'I think tea would be in order. How would that go down with you, Detective Constable Sullivan?'

Jenny very nearly said, 'Fine, I'll go and make it,' but caught herself in time.

'That would be very kind,' Harry answered for her.

Once tea was ordered and they were all seated, he took over. 'I would like to tell you what I know about your car, Mrs Wasborough. It was found in the early hours of the morning on a private road that runs between the village of Sefton Under Edge and Sefton Park. The doors were open, headlamps still on, the keys still in the ignition, and it was parked across the road. There were blood-stained fingerprints, a thumb and forefinger, on one of the windows in the driver's door. The fingerprints match those of Lady Olivia Cinders. The blood on the window is type O, Lady Olivia's blood group.'

Harry hesitated, taking the time to study the Wasboroughs' and Sir Alfred Menard's facial and body language. They barely moved. He rose from his chair and walked to the fireplace, leaning against it. Finally he spoke, addressing Caroline Wasborough. 'You are a friend of Lady Olivia's, I believe?'

'Yes, for many years,' she replied, voice steady and emotionless.

'I would very much appreciate it if you would tell me precisely what happened on the night your car vanished from this street.'

Sixsmith and Sullivan were filled with admiration for the way Harry was handling the interview. The care he took in phrasing his questions, laying on the line what he knew about her car but carefully not attacking Mrs Wasborough for withholding evidence. Sixsmith would have been more aggressive with Caroline Wasborough, and would have told her nothing of what he knew. He would have accused her of aiding and abetting a criminal and lying to Chief Inspector Pike about not even knowing the car had been stolen off the street.

'Yes, I imagine you would,' she told Harry coolly.

At that moment her houseman arrived with a massive silver tray, on it a full silver tea service and fine bone china cups and saucers.

'Do you mind if we have a cup of tea before I begin?' Caroline asked with a pleasant smile.

While she poured the tea and passed it around to everyone in the room, her husband spoke for the first time. 'I would like your word, Detective Chief Inspector, that what is said here today will not appear in the press?'

'I can promise you nothing until I've heard what you have to say. Only then will I know if that's possible,' said

Harry, taking note that Mr Wasborough looked to his solicitor for approval.

'Giles, it has to be told, and exactly as it happened. You must take your chances that the Detective Chief Inspector will understand your request and comply,' advised Sir Alfred.

'Mrs Wasborough?' said Harry.

Caroline Wasborough knew from the tone of the Chief Inspector's voice that he would wait no longer to hear what she had to say. She took a sip of tea then placed her cup and saucer on the table in front of her.

'I'll begin at the beginning. It was around eleven o'clock in the evening. My husband and I were in bed reading but Giles had fallen asleep. I heard the front door bell and then someone knocking at the door. There was nothing unusual about that. Friends often drop by on their way to Annabelle's or The Claremont round the corner in Berkeley Square. It was rare for us to be in bed so early and all our friends knew that.

'I had given Rivers the night off so it was up to me to answer the door. I did so from the upstairs hall through the intercom. It was Olivia. She sounded odd, quite agitated. She said, "Caroline, thank the Lord you're in! I need a tremendous favour – can you lend me your car?" "Come in," I told her. Then she seemed to panic. I buzzed her in but she refused, saying, "I can't come in. Something dreadful has happened and I don't want to involve you in it. I hesitate even to ask for your car but I must get out of London."

'My first thought was that she had had one of her terrible rows with Prince Ali. I knew if Olivia was on the run from him then she'd be terrified what he might do if he caught her. And so was I. He did give her the most dreadful time, but she was caught in his web and seemed unable to give him up. It was much the same with him.'

'You're digressing, darling,' said her husband.

Harry gave him a nasty look. Caroline Wasborough was giving him more information than he had so far had from any of Olivia's other friends.

'Please go on, Mrs Wasborough,' he said.

'There isn't really much more to tell. "When will you return it?" I asked. She said, "I won't. Someone will call and tell you where it is. Just pretend it was stolen and you didn't even know it." I asked her when I would see her and she replied, "This is the long goodbye. Forgive me, Caroline."

'My heart went out to her. She sounded so desperate. I told her to wait there, I would throw the car keys out of the window. I found the keys then realised that she might need some money so I went to the upstairs window and asked her if that was the case. She said, "Oh, I hadn't thought about that. Yes, as much as you can spare."

'It was then that I realised that Olivia was more than desperate, she was in real danger of losing her life. I ran back to the bedroom and was about to wake Giles when I realised I was wasting time so I opened the wall safe in the bedroom and removed two bundles of bank notes. I put them in a shoe bag along with the keys to my car. I ran to the window and tossed them down to Olivia. I don't know why I said it but my last words to her were, "Go to the police, they'll protect you."

'She laughed through her tears and replied, "Oh, darling, for the rest of my life they're my enemies. Bless you for being here for me when I needed a friend. If anyone asks, you haven't seen me, didn't even know your car was missing. Someone will call and let you know where it is. Contact my solicitor, Sir Jonathan Cowett, about the money. He'll return it to you." She threw me a kiss and was gone.

'I couldn't get to sleep for worrying about her. It had all happened so fast. A matter of what – five, ten minutes? Hardly enough time to work out just what danger she was in or indeed if she was in any real danger at all. She was just a friend in desperate need, I automatically came to her aid.

'When Giles woke in the morning, I told him exactly what had happened. He was very upset for Olivia and like myself believed she had been running away from Prince Ali. We both felt rather relieved that she had made the move at last and believed she was in fear of her life. He agreed the best way to stay out of the affair was to do as Olivia had asked. We knew her to be an amusing, charming girl but never frivolous. Olivia had always been a good and generous person, an honourable lady, an enchantress liked if not loved by everyone.'

For the first time Harry interrupted Caroline to ask, 'And when did you learn that she was suspected of murdering her lover, Prince Ali?'

'When Giles took the dogs out for a stroll round Berkeley Square. He picked up the morning papers and returned home to make us breakfast, something he does every morning. We were horrified to learn from the press what had happened. It became more understandable why Olivia was so determined not to enter the house and speak to us. She didn't want us to be dragged into the scandal. And, of course, hadn't the time to spare to explain her side of things.'

'We never told our friends that she had appeared here the night she ran away, and certainly had no intention of revealing it to the police. We made a deliberate decision to say nothing. We regret nothing. Eventually we took advice from Sir Alfred who said that if the police were to get around to questioning us, we must tell the whole truth. And so now you have it,' said Giles.

'You do know that we can charge you for withholding evidence, aiding and abetting a criminal?' put in a seriously angry Joe Sixsmith. Harry gave him a withering look.

'Will you charge my clients, Detective Chief Inspector?' queried Sir Alfred.

'Just a few more questions, Mrs Wasborough,' Harry said, addressing Caroline and ignoring Sir Alfred.

Caroline looked at her solicitor. He nodded, indicating that she should answer the Detective Chief Inspector. 'You have nothing to hide, my dear.'

'If we had not found you, you would not have come forward. Is that not so, Mrs Wasborough?'

'That is true,' she answered.

'Because you, like your friends, made the decision to close ranks, to give Olivia time to get away.'

'Yes. It's what you do when a friend needs your

support and time to do what she must to get out of a terrible situation. One hopes Olivia will one day return of her own volition and fight to clear her name.'

'How much money was in the shoe bag, Mrs Wasborough?'

'Ten thousand pounds,' answered Giles.

'She won't get far on that. We have all her assets frozen. Unless, of course, she has other friends like you to help her on her way. We will find her and justice will be done,' said Harry.

No one in the room could possibly have missed the fear and shock in the faces of Olivia's friends brought on by the words: 'We will find her and justice will be done.' Sixsmith imagined what they were saying to themselves, 'No, that will never happen, you bastards.'

Harry turned to Sir Alfred and told him, 'I will not bring a case against your clients. I see no purpose in it since I believe Mrs Wasborough came to the aid of her friend without any knowledge of Lady Olivia's involvement in the murder of her lover.'

He rose from his chair and shook hands with the Wasboroughs and Sir Alfred. 'And the press?' asked Caroline.

'They'll hear nothing from us, you have my word.'

Everyone else shook hands and Giles Wasborough and Sir Alfred insisted on seeing them out. As Giles opened the door to the street, he turned to Harry and asked, 'There's been no sign of her?'

'No. She has vanished without a trace,' answered Harry.

'One does rather fear that she may do the honourable

thing after killing Ali,' murmured Giles.

'And what would that be, Mr Wasborough, if not to turn herself in to the police?'

'Why, fall on her sword, so to speak. If indeed she has not already done so,' Giles Wasborough declared.

Chapter 5

Chief Inspector Fred Pike had got to know the landlord of The Fox when he and his men had been crawling over the village, Sefton Park and the woods, looking for clues as to who had abandoned the car there. Jethroe felt that Fred had done a fine job with little upheaval and that was good enough for him. It seemed a thing of the past and tame stuff compared to the frenzied headlines in the newspapers about Olivia. Now they were saying that there was more than enough proof she had done the murder. But the abandoned car seemed to be one case and Olivia's disappearance quite another.

Fred Pike had not revealed to him that he had found a link between the abandoned car and the missing woman. Ex-police officer, one of the fraternity and all that, meant little to Fred. He'd seen Jethroe close up like everyone else in the village when asked about the car. He, like the others in Sefton Under Edge and the Park, had given not one iota of real help to the Oxford Chief Inspector and could expect none in return.

Now Fred leaned back in his chair. He had tricked Jethroe and had no idea why he'd enjoyed that so much, though enjoy it he certainly had. He tapped the telephone with his finger and smiled. Their conversation had been simple and to the point because Fred knew that if he had told him he wanted to rent the three bedrooms above the pub for an indefinite length of time for officers from New Scotland Yard, Jethroe would have said they were fully booked. People in the village were not the type to welcome in the outside world if it was going to disrupt their peaceful existence.

And there was something else. The postman had reported to the Chief Inspector that on the morning he found the car there was a stranger with Jethroe's dogs, and that the pub owner never ordinarily let anyone use them.

Fred had gone down to London to see Harry Graves-Jones who had taken him around and introduced him to a large and impressive investigative team who congratulated him on making the connection between the car and the disappearance of Lady Olivia. Fred had been impressed, had had no idea it was such a huge man-hunt. Now it seemed that if they were ever going to pick up their suspect's trail it would be in Sefton Under Edge.

He had thought that Harry, Joe Sixsmith and Jenny Sullivan would work out of Oxford and had been disappointed when Harry insisted he wanted to set up in the village. Which had, of course, meant the pub. After greeting Jethroe on the telephone, Fred said, 'How's business? Your rooms all booked up?'

'No, but we're really busy in the pub.'

'Well, that's great. So you've got three bedrooms, mate, haven't you?'

'Yeah, and an upstairs sitting-room.'

'Perfect. I'd like to book them from tonight for an indefinite period of time. Name of Graves-Jones. Friends from London. I'll be seeing you. Gotta go.'

Jethroe put the receiver down and drank the remainder of some strong coffee laced with Scotch. It had to be New Scotland Yard men, and it had to be about Olivia. They were bound to find out that Sefton Under Edge had been her hideaway from London life. While on the one hand he resented being tricked by Fred Pike, on the other it made his adrenaline run faster to think of having New Scotland Yard in the village and watching them work at close quarters. Once a policeman not necessarily always a policeman, especially when it came to his pub, his village and the people in it for whom he cared. Jethroe laughed aloud. Yes, he would befriend the London men. But he would see to it that they learned nothing useful from him or the other inhabitants of the village.

He dialled several local numbers as he always did to summon extra help when the bedrooms were let. In the kitchen he told Selina Mayberry, the pub cook, and her assistant, Chippy Cosby, that the rooms had been let. There were no sighs but rather smiles. The staff were always happier when Jethroe had rented the rooms. The publican rarely had less than interesting guests and in their company seemed to rise to becoming the perfect landlord.

In general, Jethroe was admired by the village, for the pub was as much a centre of its daily life as anywhere else. Not everyone agreed with Jethroe's lifestyle but no one disliked him either. He was generous, protective of the village and his neighbours, a friendly, outgoing man. In a community as small as Sefton Under Edge the residents knew everything that went on in the village and lived comfortably with one another, a kindly extended family, yet kept themselves to themselves once their front doors were closed. The community was always close and yet not indissolubly so; polite, charming, careful never to offend. There was not a soul in the village who did not appreciate Jethroe's determination to run his pub very nearly like a private country club, and never to commercialise it to the point of offending the village.

It was mostly men who reserved his rooms, fishermen to whom he rented a rod, or guns joining the Buchanan shoot. The odd famous writer had been nourished by his beer and his excellent food in between tapping the keys. There was no doubt about it: Jethroe, a sometime detective, with a passion for the flute, Shakespeare and the pursuits of a country gentleman, was an asset to his community, and he had not the least intention of allowing the New Scotland Yard men to ride roughshod over his village or upset anyone.

As it happened he need not have worried about the intrusion of the detectives. They were more keen than the publican that they should make themselves evident but at the same time keep a low profile.

It was a glorious Oxfordshire morning when Joe Sixsmith drove over the little stone hump-backed bridge on the way into the village of Sefton Under Edge. The woods to either side of the narrow road were enchanting, the whole place anything but what he'd expected. He felt like an intruder into a privileged rural idyll that seemed a million light years away from sex, murder, and a woman on the run.

Sixsmith had mixed emotions about setting up a temporary office here. He already missed his London colleagues, the constant faxes, blinking computers, cacophony of telephones, even the endless paperwork and display boards listing sightings of Lady Olivia. It was a huge investigation and he'd wound up in this pretty but undeniably quiet backwater. It was hard to believe they'd make any breakthrough here.

The team arrived in two cars. The second, a four-seater cream-coloured Borgward Izabella with navy blue leather seats, usually driven by Detective Chief Inspector Harry Graves-Jones, pulled up behind Sixsmith. He watched Jenny and the Chief step out of it and he had to smile. There was no doubt about it: his boss had real style. The subtlety of that vintage car, its smooth curved lines. No, there was nothing flashy about Harry Graves-Jones. Sixsmith often drove the Borgward Izabella for him, had been a bit miffed that Harry had allowed Jenny to drive it to Oxfordshire this time, but then you couldn't stay out of sorts with the Chief for long. Often Sixsmith had wondered what made the Chief Inspector tick. It was an enigma he knew he would never crack. Not long after Jenny had joined their team, Sixsmith had told her: 'Don't try and work him out, he's just one of those special human beings you measure yourself by. I'll tell you one thing, though: every day you'll learn to raise yourself a little higher.'

'You check us in, Jenny, and book a table for lunch at

one o'clock. Select your rooms and set us up. We want our computers, fax and the direct line to the Yard up and running as soon as possible, with no fuss. Keep a low profile. I'm off for a walk. Any problems or if you need anything, call Fred Pike. But I don't want him roaring round here. In fact, I don't want him here at all until we need extra manpower. You need anything, like electrics or a telephone engineer, ask the publican. Keep our presence more cosy than official.'

Jethroe liked Joe Sixsmith from the moment he entered the pub, sighting him at once as one of the New Scotland Yard people. About thirty and dressed pretty dapper for a copper. Was he a nancy boy? But then he saw the way Sixsmith looked at Hannah the barmaid, polishing glasses at the bar, and knew he was not for sure. Sixsmith came up to him and introduced himself then Jenny to the publican. They all shook hands.

There was no one in the pub as yet other than the staff and Jethroe. Sixsmith told it like it was, 'We're setting up here in your pub,' and took out his ID to flash it under Jethroe's eyes.

'Who're you investigating?' he asked, although he knew very well it had to be Olivia.

'Look, Mr Wiley, we want to be as discreet as possible about what we're doing here. My boss is out strolling around the village now. I think you'd better ask him on his return. But in the meantime we have a hell of a lot of equipment to get up and running. Can you give us a hand?'

That was all it took. Jethroe was intrigued. Liked the

idea of being once more on the fringes, a voyeur police-man, part of the detective's game. He very nearly forgot he had no intention of allowing Olivia to be captured, any more than anyone else in the village did. Not that any of them had come out and said as much. They hadn't needed to.

Jethroe's perverse nature was amused. He saw himself as a double agent, so to speak, playing the law at its own game to make sure Olivia was safe. Then for a few minutes he forgot about playing games and felt cut to the heart, the very soul, because he knew instinctively he would never see or hear from her again.

Harry Graves-Jones greeted several people on his tour of the village. They rightly assumed he was one of The Fox's guests. There was something more romantic than chocolate-box English countryside about the place. Its situation was certainly beautiful but far from a stereo-type. Life here seemed to be idyllic but lived in slow motion. Harry passed the school house and was impressed to see it was still in use though closed for the summer holiday.

In a back street he came upon a butcher's shop and smiled at the sight of the butcher with his straw boater. Two cars arrived one after the other and he watched a pair of elderly couples enter the shop. The greengrocer's was across the narrow cobbled street and Harry saw that the stock was all organically grown by local market gardens.

Back in the centre of the village, he saw several people with shopping baskets over their arms, a few toddlers who should have seemed out of place but didn't. A tall, slender woman with jet black hair tied back in a chiffon scarf caught his eye. A floppy bow at her ear sprang up and down with her every stride. She was dressed in a thin white linen dress and the sun behind her outlined a slender yet sensuous body. Life, passion, an awareness of self, seemed to be pumping through her veins like blood. Now *she* was more like a reason for Olivia to seek help here than anything he had seen so far.

The woman wore no make-up save for her dramatically accentuated almond-shaped eyes. She seemed to emanate power and intelligence and there was about her a sexiness that spoke of freedom and joy. It made Harry smile.

He had been sitting close to the edge of the pond on an old weather-worn bench, enjoying the sun and thinking of Olivia. Who had come to her aid in this village? Instinct told him someone or some group of people had spirited her away from this place. Who would be so devoted to her that they would risk a criminal conviction for aiding and abetting a murderer?

Harry rose from the bench and started walking towards the eastern beauty striding into the village from the direction in which the abandoned car had been found. Their eyes met and Harry recognised the woman as being a famous feminist writer and academic who had forged herself a huge career as writer and media pundit with a brand of casuistry that periodically turned male theories upside down. A rebel with a perennial cause. That made his smile even wider.

Would that he could remember her name. He had, on

the few times he had heard her on those intellectual chat shows aired at midnight, found her fifty per cent charlatan and one hundred per cent intelligent. She was one of the new breed of women who had inherited their rights from the seventies activists and now that they had them didn't quite know what to do with them. He liked and admired her and now, seeing her without an audience to impress, just strolling in the sunshine, he thought she might be fun to interview as well as a very plausible suspect who just might have whisked Lady Olivia away to a safe haven.

Harry stopped her with a, 'Good morning.'

'Hello,' said Marguerite with a broad smile.

'Will you have coffee with me at Miss Marble's tea room?' he asked.

'Well, I am rather fond of her drop scones. I usually have them around eleven every morning that I come into the village, but only after I feed the ducks in the pond. I might agree if I know who you are,' she told him as she walked away towards the water. Harry followed.

From the basket of stale bread and cake she was carrying, Marguerite tossed pieces on to the water. He reached into her basket and took a handful too. 'Do you mind?' he asked before tossing it on the water. 'My name is Harry Graves-Jones and I'm staying at the pub for a few days.'

'Cambridge,' she guessed.

'That's very good. How did you know?'

'Linguistic analysis – and your college tie,' she told him, laughing.

'Not mine, my dead uncle's, but I *did* go to Cambridge.'

'So did I. That's good enough for me to accept an

71

invitation to coffee. My name is Marguerite Chen.'

There was something immensely attractive about this stranger, she thought, not only physically but in the way he carried himself. He was wearing a blue shirt, the college tie, and a waistcoat of Harris tweed over grey flannel trousers with turn-ups. There was an ease about him that was madly attractive and she felt instantly that he was something special, that one in a hundred thousand you actually wanted to meet.

By now the ducks had come up to her and Marguerite squatted down and fed them by hand. Harry joined her and before long they were laughing together and feeding the endearing creatures who were madly quacking and fluttering their wings. They teased and tantalised Marguerite, one even pulling at the chiffon bow over her ear and running off with a banner of purple streaming behind him.

'The little bastard got me! I call him Wolfgang. He's the really feisty one who's always trying to snatch something from me. My guard must have been down today. He never succeeds usually.'

They watched Wolfgang drag the chiffon scarf over the surface of the pond. Marguerite turned over the contents of the basket then slipped her arm through Harry's, announcing, 'Come on, you can row the boat. I *really* like that scarf.'

Half an hour later the limp wet scarf was safely in her basket and they were walking arm in arm into Miss Marble's tea room. There were half a dozen people already sitting at the small cream-clothed tables with garden flowers in small glass vases at their centre.

They sat down at a table in the window after Marguerite had introduced Harry to Miss Marble as someone staying for a few days at the pub. Harry, who had a passion for marvellous sweets, puddings and cakes, was surprised by what was on offer. There were pedestal cake plates proffering luscious-looking triple-layered cakes covered in chocolate, each layer spread thick with apricot jam, lemon tarts, glazed fruit tarts, a coffee cream cake, strawberry cream cake . . . The choice seemed to go on forever.

'I'm spoiled for choice,' he told Miss Marble.

The plain-looking grey-haired lady smiled with delight as she told him, 'Yes, they come from far and wide for tea and cake here. The Americans, in particular, want to taste it all so we do a special taster – small portions of various cakes. How would you like to try that? One doesn't like to admit it, but those Americans are so much more adventurous than we English in their eating habits. And for you, Marguerite, the drop scones, I presume? Our Marguerite likes those.'

Marguerite seemed to be much admired in the village. Harry found it interesting the way everyone in the tea room gave a pleasant nod and a smile but no one intruded on their privacy. Once seated, and without any discernible reason, an awkward silence descended upon Marguerite and Harry. She found it somewhat irritating, this awkward small talk that invariably results between two people who have just met.

Harry was aware of her change of expression. 'That was fun, feeding the ducks and retrieving your scarf. I've always had a real fondness for ducks ever since I was a child.'

Marguerite felt the warmth of his smile and knew he was telling her she had given him a good time, childlike, which was something he rarely had any more. 'I think it's strange you should have come away on a break wearing your tie. Undo it and open your shirt collar, kick off your shoes so to speak, or I might think you've come here for some other reason.'

It was said in jest and with a smile. She was quite surprised when he did nothing of the sort. 'That's quite astute. Are you always so observant?' he asked.

Sarah Marble brought the tray of tea and a cake stand to the table. It was a little too much for her to handle. Marguerite was instantly on her feet and helping to serve. But the moment Miss Marble left them she sat down and looked directly into Harry's eyes, 'Yes, that's the sort of mind I have,' she admitted, while pouring coffee into his cup from a silver pot.

She sat back in her chair, still looking at him, and said, 'You're here for more than the trout fishing, and that bothers me.'

'Why?'

'Because I dislike disruption – handsome strangers with inquisitive minds who drop into my world and shuffle it around. I'm getting the distinct feeling that this is what's happening here.'

'I hope to make it as painless as possible for everyone,' he said.

Marguerite was stunned by that answer. She felt fear coil in the pit of her stomach. 'Would you mind expanding on that?'

'I'm actually Detective Chief Inspector Harry Graves-

Jones, here with two colleagues from New Scotland Yard, leading an investigation into the disappearance of Lady Olivia Cinders.'

'You might have said,' she told him testily, unable to hide her disapproval.

'But I *am* saying,' he replied, and forked a piece of cake into his mouth.

Marguerite buttered her scone and placed a dollop of peach preserve on it. It was delicious, she was sure, but it tasted like ashes in her mouth. The two of them remained silent while they ate, occasionally looking out of the window.

'Are you never going to talk to me again?' Harry asked, somewhat teasingly.

'Why has that tragic case suddenly arrived on our doorstep?' Marguerite answered his question with one of her own.

'The abandoned car that was found here was easy to trace. It belonged to a Mrs Caroline Wasborough. After a number of days a clever detective made the link between the abandoned car and Lady Olivia. Her finger-prints were all over it. Either with or without another person she drove the car here, presumably to ask for help to get away. Sefton Under Edge is our only break so far in the case. We know for sure that she was here and we mean to pick up her trail. You do know Lady Olivia Cinders, don't you?'

'Don't bother unpacking, Detective Chief Inspector. If Olivia had been here looking for help, she would have come to me. And she didn't.'

'Call me Harry – I think we like each other enough to

call each other by our first names. Olivia went to someone for help in this village, Marguerite, and that someone spirited her away from here.'

'So you say. I tell you, it's not possible. The night in question a group of us were together partying at Sefton Park, her closest and dearest, and in the case of the Buchanans her oldest friends. We knew nothing of the abandoned car until the following day when the postman discovered it, blocking the road to the Park. If she did drive it here why did she abandon it in that odd manner across the road? She must have changed her mind, deciding not to involve us. She might even have left it here as a decoy while she made her getaway.'

'Marguerite, someone in this village has duped you. They have done the deed and until now never revealed what they did to another living soul. Silence was and is Olivia's only hope. They know that, and anyone who wants to aid and abet her knows it. So do you. Think about it, Marguerite, think about it hard. What sort of life can Olivia hope for, on the run for the rest of her life? We're after her and mean to get her but the prince's family are mounting a private search for her and you know what they'll put her through if they find her before I do. Help me to learn what she's like so that I can find her and bring her to justice. It's her only hope.'

'You call that hope? That's a hope made in hell. And Olivia wasn't made for hell. She couldn't stand going to prison. Probably why she fled in the first place. And I'll tell you something else: tread carefully with us here in this village. You may turn over stones and reveal more than any of us wants to become public knowledge.'

'Why are you so angry with me? Surely not because I'm hunting down your friend for taking a life. I heard you once declare to a TV audience that there was no greater crime than taking a human life. It makes redemption impossible. Or have you changed your mind about that now that it's your friend Lady Olivia who's in the dock? You know, my dear, you're a good thinker and a joy to listen to because you make people contemplate serious issues, but you're not always honest and certainly not always right. Seventy-five per cent twaddle, ten per cent charm, and the rest fine scholarship and intellect. That's a back-handed compliment, I know, but it's meant to tell you I respect who and what you are and are not. I promise to tread carefully on people's toes but, by God, like it or not, you *will* answer my queries. Now have a taste of this cake, it's delicious.'

Marguerite rose from her chair, saying, 'You're an insulting bastard.'

'No, an honest officer of the law,' he told her as he rose to kiss her hand. Then, very softly, whispered: 'Don't play games with me. Be my friend, not my enemy, and have dinner with me in the pub this evening?'

Without answering him, she walked away.

Chapter 6

Marguerite was angry. The New Scotland Yard man was spot on in his assessment of her. She knew it, many of her critics had said the same things about her and had done so since she first came on the scene fifteen years before. Women listened as much to her now as they had ever done. But she was flawed and so were many of her philosophies. She had allowed her ambition and intelligence to trample on her ability to *love* a man for no other reason than *love* (the weak woman's anaesthetic to self-development). A deep genuine love that made no demands except to be in it had been for her too demeaning, or at least she'd thought so until she met Olivia, who was love incarnate. Marguerite simply could not bear to give herself up totally and with a generous heart to a man; she had never found one good enough to receive such a gift. Oh, yes, for great sex, orgasmic ecstasy. To soar with a man for a few seconds. She did that well and often. But it was short-lived ecstasy and in constant need of feeding.

Who was this Harry Graves-Jones? He was someone special with a keen intelligence, a man who didn't suffer fools easily. Over no more than a cup of coffee he'd had the measure of her, and if he was that quick with her he was bound to be no less so with all concerned with Olivia. It was going to be tough trying to protect their privacy, their lifestyle, to keep their secrets and most especially Olivia's. And where the hell was she anyway? Beautiful, wonderful Olivia, gone from their lives forever? This Harry Graves-Jones, had he met her, would be no different than any of them – in love with her. That made Marguerite smile. Harry was just the sort of man Olivia could and would seduce. He already seemed enthralled by her and had not even laid eyes on her yet. How long, she wondered, before he would forget his pursuit of justice? Marguerite hurried home to call James and warn him who was in their midst.

Harry remained in Miss Marble's tea shop long after Marguerite had walked out on him. He was aware that he had been quite hard on her but it had been necessary. He had no intention of deceiving her or anyone else in the village about his reason for being here. Marguerite was a woman of too much charm, too clever in the art of manipulation, and he wanted her to realise she could not fool him. Now she did.

Miss Marble interrupted his contemplation. 'Another cup of coffee, Mr Graves-Jones?'

Harry looked around the tea room. He was the only customer left in it. The young waitress was busy resetting tables. He rose from his chair and asked, 'If you will join me, Miss Marble.'

She was charmed by his good looks, recognised him as a gentleman, and he obviously loved her cakes which was flattering. 'I'm not intruding?' she asked.

'Not in the least,' was his reply.

After ordering Annie to bring another pot of coffee for Harry and tea for herself, she sat down. 'The Americans always ask if I would like to join them but you're my first Englishman,' she said somewhat shyly.

'Miss Marble, you are a master pastry chef,' he complimented her. She beamed. 'I expect to be here in Sefton Under Edge for several days so you and I will be seeing each other every day.'

Delight was clear in her face. 'Are you here for fishing? The stream is well known for its blue trout. The gillie has a smoke house downstream and you've never tasted anything like it when he's smoked the catch – the flesh looks like smoked salmon and tastes wonderful,' she said.

'Well, maybe I can get some of that in but the real reason I'm here is because I am a Detective Chief Inspector from New Scotland Yard, in charge of the Lady Olivia Cinders case.'

'Oh, I do hope our Olivia is all right! I'm certain there must be a mistake.'

'Do you know her?'

'Have done all her life. The loveliest girl in England. And such a lady. She's one of those rare people one occasionally comes across for whom one would lay down one's life without a qualm. She and the Buchanan girls grew up together. They're like family. And the lovely men who used to come here with her! You just never met anyone so full of life and laughter – and bright as a penny. Of course, she went to Oxford. I make all her birthday cakes and Sir James delivers them to the most exotic places. We pack them in his plane and off he goes.'

'Miss Marble, does Sir James fly his own plane?'

'Several, and he has his own private airstrip. Maybe he'll take you up. He's very generous about that. Loves to fly. Marguerite keeps a plane here too, and the Buchanan girls, September and Angelica. They live a very sophisticated life up at the Park with marvellous grown-up toys: planes and vintage cars and so on. They have a fantastic life here with their friends and are always doing things for the village. A few years ago I had pneumonia. Do you know, Olivia and James flew the bread and pastry up from London, fresh each day, and she and September ran the tea room.'

Miss Marble leaned forward and whispered across the table, 'I don't know how they did it but I made more money when those girls were running the shop than I've ever done before my illness or since.'

'Does Olivia have her own plane?'

'Oh, no, she uses the Buchanans'.'

'Does she have a house here?'

'No, she lives at Sefton Park. You know, Detective Chief Inspector, you must clear Olivia's name, you really must.'

'Well, I have to find her first, Miss Marble.'

'Is that why you've come? Oh, you won't find her here.'

'Yes, that's why I'm here. And why are you so sure Olivia isn't hiding out in someone's house locally?'

Miss Marble said quite seriously, 'Because we have

looked everywhere for her in the hope of finding and helping her. We've been talking endlessly to one another about why she hasn't come. We worry about her, living in fear and with no friends. She must know we'd help her but Olivia quite obviously doesn't want to involve us in her problem. I have no doubt that as soon as she's over the shock of what's happened, she'll go to you of her own accord.'

Harry found his chat with Miss Marble strangely unreal. Did no one understand that the woman he was hunting was a murderer? Did they not understand that there was overwhelming evidence that this young woman they had adored, and still did, had a dark side to her that allowed her to take a man's life? Did they not think of the prince, the law of the land, anything except how much they loved and admired Olivia?

In the pub Harry introduced himself to Jethroe Wiley and then went up to his room. He was an hour on the telephone checking out the latest sightings from Interpol. 'Anything to report before we go down to lunch?' he asked the team.

'Give us a chance, sir. We've been setting ourselves up all morning. And the e-mail and faxes are non-stop.'

'Quite so. Forget the phones for a few minutes. Let's go over what we've learned since our arrival. Fact, Olivia drove that car here. Fact, she had good reason. This was her village, the place she felt at home. Fact, her best friends live here. Fact, she lived at Sefton Park from time to time. Very important fact, she knows how to fly a plane. Fact, there's a private airstrip a fifteen-minute walk from here where several planes are kept. Fact,

Marguerite Chen lives here and is a friend of Lady Olivia's. Fact, Miss Marble from the tea shop speaks of Olivia as a saint.

'I think we're in the right place to find out all we can about the real Lady Olivia but the wrong place to catch her. Instinct tells me she's long since fled abroad and the only way we'll find her is to gather information about what happened on the night the car was abandoned. To come to know and understand Lady Olivia Cinders so well we can anticipate her every move and follow every lead we uncover. Fact, time is no longer on our side and of course she might possibly be dead. Jenny, what have you got, if anything?'

'No facts, sir, but I'm suspicious of the publican and the barmaid, Hannah Brite. I'd like to be the one to interview them, sir.'

'Always follow up your suspicions, Sullivan. What about you, Sixsmith?'

'The publican is a retired policeman. He's been a great help to me, sir, but there *is* something strange about him. The way he speaks to the barmaid. Something in his manner. This pub is his world and so's the village, apparently. He's dropped more than one hint that he doesn't want us upsetting things. The way he looks at Jenny, I think he must be a real womaniser,' reported Sixsmith.

'And not a very nice one,' she added.

'And other than that?' asked Harry.

'Nothing. He's a genuine character and according to Hannah is the heartbeat of the village. Everyone likes Jethroe Wiley whose generosity is well known.'

'I'll take Jethroe. This is going to have to be a house-to-house investigation. Remember, we want to know the truth about Lady Olivia, flaws and all, so we can build up a picture of this woman. Knowing her as well as she does herself is the way we'll pick up her trail.'

In the pub they took their table. The place was already filled with people – drinking, laughing, dining. It was a marked contrast to the morning when the clientele was more sparse and only called in briefly. When Hannah Brite brought them their main course of trout almandine on a bed of buttered spinach and a mountain of French fried potatoes, a bowl of fresh garden vegetables au gratin cooked to perfection, Harry could see how special the place was and that Jethroe drew his custom from the surrounding villages as well as his own.

It was evident from the look on people's faces, the whispers and glances directed at Harry and his team, that word of who they were and why they were here was now common knowledge. Their meal finished, the three of them separated. Harry headed for Sefton Park to interview the Buchanans.

Passing through the gates of the park and up the winding drive, the ruins of the once great Tudor house and what was left and conserved of Sefton Park, cast a spell over Harry that compelled him to pull up the car and cut the motor. He stepped out of it and felt a glorious soft, warm breeze carrying the scent of acres of the brightest green grass, and from somewhere close by the scent of roses and wild flowers. He walked in the direction of the ruins and was rewarded by the sight of a folly-sized version of Sefton Park. This was privilege on a grand scale; this was Olivia, her lifestyle. He could imagine her riding across the parkland, full of spirit and the joy of life. He could feel her presence all around him. She wasn't dead. A girl who was so much a part of this world would have taken her chance, not fallen on her sword as Giles Wasborough had suggested.

Relief washed over Harry. Lady Olivia Cinders was still alive, and had been very clever in her getaway. So far he had felt it had been an accidental killing, a sex game gone wrong. Now he was not so sure. Lady Olivia's getaway had been carefully planned, possibly only after the deed had been done but planned nevertheless.

Harry's thoughts were interrupted by the sight of a beautiful horse ridden at full gallop through one of the massive stone Tudor arches and down the grassy hillock towards him: a palomino with a long cream-coloured mane streaming into the wind, tail swishing with wild enthusiasm from side to side. The rider was young, no more than in her early twenties. She had long chestnut-coloured hair that shone in the sun and when she pulled up in front of Harry, he saw large blue eyes sparkling with life. She wore riding clothes but no hat and as she slung one leg over her horse and leaped to the ground he liked what he saw of her figure: slender and small-breasted. She was stunning and enormously sensuous. Her body language was erotic, face young and innocent with a voluptuous mouth and bee-stung upper lip.

She had about her the aura of one who is free in love, a winner. Just the sort of young girl he liked to make love to, enjoyed having on his arm as well as in his bed.

It was a strange thing for him to do but she was irresistible. Harry placed his hands on his hips and leaned back on his heels, laughing aloud. She smiled because he was enjoying her so much. There was something really exciting about him; she was overtaken by an overwhelming desire to have sex with him. His good looks were only a part of it. There was a strength and a sweetness to his manner, a sexual charisma too strong to hide from. September wanted him to take her, hit the heights of sexual bliss and beyond. Without a word being uttered between them, she had fallen in love. She had never felt for another man what she felt for this stranger. Her first words to him were, 'Are you married?'

Her voice was husky and sensuous and there was a teasing note in it. Or so he thought. He learned different after he had answered, 'No.'

September smiled and Harry thought his heart would melt. 'That's great,' she told him.

She handed him the reins to her horse and swung herself up into the saddle, extending her hand, 'I never get involved with a man who's already spoken for. Too much pain.'

Harry handed her the reins then took her hand and swung himself up on the horse behind her. He slid his arms around her waist and they started at a slow trot over the parkland. September leaned back against his chest and was thrilled by the warmth of his body. Harry ran his fingers through her hair then brushed it off the nape of her neck and kissed it. He licked her ear lobes and September felt herself giving in to him. He unbuttoned her blouse and she wriggled out of it. Harry caressed her breasts, her shoulders, down her naked arms and around her midriff. She could feel him hard against her.

'This is madness but wonderful madness, the kind that dreams and fantasies are made of,' he whispered in her ear.

'That love is made of. Love for no other reason than being one with another human being,' she told him.

She pulled the horse up and, turning in the saddle to look over her shoulder, continued, 'You're not a criminal of any sort, are you?'

He laughed and told her, 'Certainly not. I take it that makes two sorts of men you don't have sex with?'

September turned round to face forward. He felt her stiffening in his arms. He sensed he had upset her with his teasing and felt simply dreadful. He could hardly understand this desire to have outrageous sex with her but also to love and protect her from hurt. And he didn't even know her name. He simply could not leave it at that, he had to tell her and he did.

'You have to know I will never hurt you. Never tease you like that again. I only want to be a joy in your life, for us to build something out of instant passion, that crazy thing, love at first sight.'

Harry was close to tears. He had found someone who was the other half of himself. It had never happened to him before and he had never thought it would. He understood the passion she felt for him, that the love that had burst upon them was something akin to a special kind of nirvana. They were meant for each other.

'Yes,' she said. He could hear the tension in her voice

along with a sweetness and a passion that were impossible to miss. They rode the remainder of the way to the Sefton Park stables in silence. Before they entered the yard she slipped into her blouse and Harry buttoned it up for her.

Once in her bedroom in the house she locked the door and turned to face him. He raised her in his arms and kissed her face as she stripped herself of her blouse once more. He placed her on her feet and watched her pull off her riding boots and breeches. Now naked before him there was a certain sexual sophistication about her. She, like Harry, had a strong libido, no sexual fear. Lust was something she wore very well, and with pride.

Once he was naked before her she went to him, wrapped her arms around his neck and kissed him first on his lips: a deep, passionate kiss. Then she worked her way down his body, licking him with her tongue, sucking on his nipples. September was overwhelmed with lust for him and his body, his very scent excited her immeasurably, the texture of his skin inflamed her senses. To feel the weight of his phallus in her hand and cup his scrotum was overwhelming. She felt for this man as she had never before felt for another. Sex with him had nothing to do with the sex and wild sprees she and Olivia used to enjoy. It was that and more, an extra dimension of lust because of love, not instead of it.

All her life she had been attracted physically and emotionally to greatness in men. Her lovers had been good-looking, interesting, famous and creative men and women. During September and Harry's lovemaking she learned he was all those things and much more. His delight in erotic and adventurous sex was matched by her own and together they drifted from the here and now into total union where every second was a sexual bliss that kept building, breaking down the sexual taboos one after the other. Both of them were lost in lust and love. They called out in transports of ecstasy, bit into each other's flesh with a hunger more intense than they had ever felt for another human being. They licked and sucked every drop they could of each other's come so as never to forget a taste more intimate, more special and blissful, their own elixir.

When they had arrived at the stables, September had asked for the keys to Harry's car and tossed them to the stable lad, telling him to drive it to the front entrance of the house. Now, as they bathed together several hours after she had kidnapped Harry's heart, he thought of the car and how he would like to drive her to dinner and stay the night with her at a country house hotel or in the Randolph in Oxford.

Once the invitation was issued, she answered, 'Here comes the real world. I'd be just as happy sleeping with you in your room at the pub. No one would be shocked, the villagers know us to be somewhat on the wild side up here at the Park. They give us our freedom to live as we want to and we in turn try never to offend them with our indiscretions.'

Harry watched her joyously select a red silk slip dress and raw silk black jacket with very high stiletto-heeled black shoes. She overwhelmed him with her style, the sensuality she wore like a perfume. Her flush of happiness came from sexual bliss, a great deal of it, the thrill of lovemaking edged with depravity, trust and love. The very idea that this marvellous-looking, spirited woman wanted to share herself and her life with him, now and for always, was overwhelming.

Before they had risen from her bed September had told him that she had always wanted to give herself totally but he was the only man with whom it had come naturally to her, and it was more glorious than she had ever imagined. It was just there with him, this total submission to love, as simple as breathing. He confessed he felt the same way and their two hearts were beating as one.

They were walking down the grand staircase. Harry could not remember ever feeling as happy as he was at that moment. He stopped her from taking another step and turned her to face him. Feeling quite ridiculous he said, 'My name is Harry Graves-Jones.'

'Harry Graves-Jones, Harry Graves-Jones,' she repeated. 'A little late for names, Harry, since I've already made up my mind you're the man I'm going to marry. September Buchanan, that's me.'

They laughed at the situation. But almost immediately Harry sobered. September Buchanan was one of Olivia's best friends. He realised he must talk to her seriously before they left the house. 'September, is there somewhere we can talk? There's something I have to tell you.'

'Can't it wait?' she asked, wanting to remain in the blissful state she was wrapped in without the outside world impinging.

'No, I'm afraid not.'

She very nearly said, 'You don't want to marry me!'

but September was secure in herself and her instincts were usually correct so she said nothing. Harry Graves-Jones had been seduced by her into love and for as long as he lived would never fall out of it, she was as sure of that as she was certain of her love for him. So she kissed his hand and told him, 'The library.'

They had not reached the ground floor when her brother James arrived by the front door. Introductions were made and they all three went into the library. Harry took the measure of James and liked him immediately. He was handsome and there was a charm about him not unlike his sister's. Harry was impressed by the way he greeted September with a smile and a kiss. The manner in which he complimented her on looking so gloriously happy. There was an ease between them but Harry could sense respect and admiration too, a family bond he himself had only had with his uncle.

This was the happiest time of September's life and yet she did not feel compelled to blurt out her feelings, the huge change that had so suddenly come upon her. Of course she knew James could not miss her happiness and would discover for himself that she was in love. With such closeness between brother and sister it was inevitable.

'I sense a celebration or something akin to it so how about mixing us one of your cocktails, September? Say a Martini. She's a whizz at them, Harry.'

He felt himself slipping into the comfort of genuine hospitality. Sliding into feelings of wanting to belong not only to September but to this home and privileged family. But Harry had learned a very long time before how to cut off emotion and switch back to that other part of himself which dealt with the cold facts of life.

He walked over to September and led her to a worn leather wing chair by the fireplace. She was stunned by the change in him. It was not so much that all passion and love for her had vanished, more that he had drawn a veil over them. Here was another side to the man with whom she had fallen in love. She sat in the chair and he sat on its arm, holding her hand. She sensed that whatever was happening he loved her, she had no doubt of that.

He looked away from her to James and said, 'Would you mind terribly if I had a word with you both before September mixes us those drinks?'

James sat down and she asked, 'What's going on, Harry?'

He rose from the arm of the chair and walked to the fireplace. 'I am Detective Chief Inspector Harry Graves-Jones, in charge of the search for Lady Olivia Cinders.'

Neither sister nor brother said a word though September went pale. Several seconds passed during which she rose from her chair and announced, 'I think I'll make those Martinis now.'

James said, 'Olivia isn't here, Chief Inspector.'

'No, Sir James, but the night she ran away from the scene of the crime it was to here that she fled. As I am certain you already know, Marguerite Chen no doubt having told you, the abandoned car found on your private road the morning after the murder had been driven by Lady Olivia. She was here all right. And someone or several persons helped her to get away from

Sefton Under Edge. Here's where I will pick up her trail and learn what really happened that night.'

'My brother has told you – Olivia isn't here, Harry,' said September.

'But he didn't say that she hadn't been.'

'Until Marguerite told me she had been, I had no knowledge of her being here that night,' said James.

'And you had none either, September?'

'No. I only wish she *had* come to us. We would have stood by her, she knew that.'

'And spirited her away?'

'Yes, if that was all that would save her.'

September went to Harry and handed him his Martini, her hand trembling. His heart went out to her. He wanted to take her in his arms, kiss her and tell her it was all going to come right for them. He watched her drain her powerful drink almost at a gulp. She took off her jacket and flung it on a chair then went to stand by the window. A storm was brewing and rain slashed against the many panes of glass through the blackness of the night. Sometimes it beat in sheets, whipped up by the wind.

Harry addressed James. 'I'd like to interview you and your family formally, one by one, not as a group. The staff as well. I'll be here tomorrow to see you, shall we say around eleven?'

Turning to face September, he said, 'After lunch?' But did not wait for confirmation. Instead he announced, 'My assistants will conduct the staff interviews.'

September was horrified. She walked from the window to stand in front of him. Raising his hand to her lips, she kissed it, caressed his cheek and felt a rush of ecstasy at the memory of the taste of him, his power and passion as a lover. She gazed into his eyes and said, 'Let her go, Harry. You *have* to. For my sake. What hope is there for us if Olivia is hounded to her death by you?'

Chapter 7

Driving back to the village through the downpour, a vision of September walking away from him and out of the library kept flashing before Harry through the hypnotic to and fro of the windscreen wipers. She would appear from the blackness and vanish under a cascade of water into the night. The sadness in her face when he'd made no reply to her request was something he would remember all his life.

She had asked him to do something that was impossible. Had she not realised that such a demand would set them at odds? Could she not see that making such a request placed them both in an untenable position? Harry's love for September had struck him like a bolt of lightning. He was aware that it would continue to affect him all the days of his life. Had it not been exactly the same for her?

She must love Olivia beyond measure or why would September risk her newfound happiness for her friend? Olivia . . . What was this power she had over people? He could feel her seductive charm in the depths of his soul. Harry was smitten by this most unusual woman who manifested herself as a shining star everyone wanted to touch, be a part of, and was now coming between him and love on a grand scale, an erotic coupling that was unimaginably thrilling. September was already a part of Harry's life, but then again so was finding Lady Olivia Cinders whose dark side it seemed must always be forgiven. Why?

He was wet through when he entered the pub. Much to his surprise it was still filled with people. He went to the bar and asked Hannah Brite for a double whisky. The kitchen was closed but Jethroe offered to cook him a fillet steak. Harry went upstairs to change into dry clothes, then to the sitting-room where he saw Sixsmith pondering some papers. Harry liked Joe Sixsmith, had high hopes for him. He was quick of mind, often too quick and inclined to rush to judgement. But that was mostly inexperience and not being as cautious as Harry would like him to be. Sixsmith listened and learned from his mistakes and he was conscientious. They made a good team.

'What are you mulling over?' Harry asked.

'I had the Yard fax us all the information on flight plans registered by both English and French air traffic controllers, to see if we had missed anything now we have a clearer idea where Lady Olivia might have taken off from. I spoke at length with Paris Information, a radio contact point for aircraft, but they had nothing to help us. If a plane flew from the airstrip here I can tell you the pilot took a terrific chance because he failed to 'activate' his flight plan as pilots are legally required to do.'

'She could have flown herself or been flown from here, taken the dangerous chance of not activating her flight plan and not headed direct for the Channel. She could have headed for somewhere else in England and crossed the Channel by boat,' suggested Harry.

'No, I don't think so, sir. She'd choose to get out of England as fast and as far as she could. That's what I'm sure she did. With her network of friends maybe she changed planes several times. I'm following several possibilities but I have little hope. It took me three hours to get the authorities to mount an investigation of every private landing field along the coast of the south of France.'

'Every lead must be followed, Joe, but I'd bet that whoever flew Lady Olivia out of the country, a flight plan was never issued by the authorities either here or in France. If we do establish that she used the Sefton Park airstrip to get away we will pursue it to the end, you can be sure of that.'

Harry offered Joe a drink and the two men went down to the bar. Jethroe had laid a place for Harry at the end of it since all the tables were still taken, which suited him very well as it set him apart from the hustle and bustle of the patrons. Someone moved from the bar stool next to him down one without being asked and Joe took it. Harry was distracted by the extent of The Fox's wine list which gave him another insight into the pub's clientele. He ignored the several reds and whites in the lower price range and went for a bottle of red Burgundy.

Jethroe served fillet steak and paper-thin slivers of potato roasted in olive oil and rosemary and crisped to a crunchy golden brown. Harry, seeing the food, realised how hungry he was. He watched Jethroe pour the wine into their glasses and began his meal at once. Joe sat quietly drinking his wine, the two men barely exchanging a word. Mostly they listened and observed. Once Harry had finished his meal he turned round on his bar stool and drank his wine, facing the crowd of drinkers. He watched Miss Marble rise unsteadily from her chair and walk away from the group she was sitting with. He was about to go to her aid and see her home when Jethroe placed a hand on his sleeve.

'No, that would embarrass her. She drinks herself into this state every evening and we pretend not to notice. She becomes offended if we help her, so someone at her table waits until she's through the door then follows her home. They watch for the light over the bakery to go on, see her pull the curtains to then return here. We take care of each other in this village.'

Miss Marble passed by quite close to Harry. She acknowledged him with a dignified nod of her head but did not stop. It was as if she had gathered momentum and dare not. Once she was through the door he saw one of the men at her table rise and put his cap on his head, take a Barbour from the back of his chair and go after her.

Shortly after Miss Marble's exit, Harry went up to bed. He was a man who needed little sleep and hardly ever felt tired. However, this evening was an exception. He felt emotionally drained and weary to his soul. He made it to his bed and fell straight into a dreamless sleep. Upon awakening his first thought was of September. She was with him in spite of Olivia, they were already each other's world. He bathed and dressed and called down to Jethroe to say he wanted a full English breakfast and a great deal of black coffee. He found his two assistants in the sitting-room already on the telephones. 'I'll be downstairs having breakfast,' he announced.

Hannah laid a table for him. 'I think you must be an exceptional detective, not your run-of-the-mill policeman.'

'And what makes you say that?' he asked her with a smile.

'A box of small white orchids in the refrigerator for one thing,' she told him as she handed one of the blossoms to him.

'Ah, you remembered I like a fresh one every morning,' he reminded her.

'Do you mind if I ask you why you wear it. It's a very romantic thing for a detective to do.'

Harry pushed the blossom's stem through the buttonhole of his jacket and secured it with a pin. 'I have never thought it to be a romantic gesture, more a thing of beauty to behold, a reminder, if you will, to be grateful for every day and night and all the splendours of the world.'

'That's so beautiful. What an unusual man you are.'

'Measured against whom?' he asked, amused by Hannah and her questions.

'I'll go and get your breakfast,' she said looking flushed, her eyes sparkling with excitement.

She had just returned from the kitchen with Harry's breakfast when Jethroe entered the pub with his Dalmatians. He greeted Harry in a rather offhand manner, let the dogs off the leash and watched them scamper, slipping and sliding, across the worn stone floor towards the kitchen. They too wanted their breakfast.

'Hannah, mind the pub. I'm going into Oxford. Make sure you pick up the bread from Miss Marble.' And Jethroe was out of the door before she had a chance to answer him.

The barmaid placed a hot plate of bacon, eggs, sausage and fried bread in front of Harry. He noticed when she bent forward to pour steaming black coffee into his cup that there were black and blue fingermarks to either side of her neck and that her hand was trembling. He steadied it by placing his own over it. She looked into his eyes and tears were brimming in hers. Harry gently moved aside the white collar of her blouse and exposed the bruises. Hannah pulled back.

'Why don't you get yourself a cup and have some coffee with me while I have my breakfast?' he asked kindly.

She looked fearfully at the entrance to the pub to see if Jethroe was coming back. They heard his car roar off and Harry did not miss the expression of relief on her face. Hannah smiled and pulled herself up, even gave him a smile. 'I think I'll do that, if you're sure you mean it?'

When she returned with her cup and saucer she was carrying a plate of hot buttered toast. Harry forked some bacon and egg into his mouth and Hannah spread a piece of the toast with gooseberry jam and bit into it.

'Those bruises on your neck look fresh, would you like to tell me about them?' he asked.

102

Hannah placed her hand on the offending marks then pulled her collar forward to cover them. 'Only if you promise to do nothing about what I tell you? You being a policeman and all.'

'I promise if that's what you want,' he answered, thinking how pretty and sexy she was.

'I don't see why you shouldn't know. It's common knowledge that I'm Jethroe's girlfriend and that when he gets drunk he sometimes gets violent with me. You were sure to find out sooner or later.'

'Why do you stand for it?'

'Because I love him and it doesn't happen all the time. It's kind of a sexual thing, or partly. And most of the time it's set off by something I do or say.'

'He must stop or you must leave him, Hannah. This isn't good for either of you.'

'Oh, I couldn't do that! I tried a couple of times and I was miserable without him. It's just the way it is, the way *he* is, and not all the time. Our sex life is just one of the many skeletons in the closet here at Sefton Under Edge. We all know each other's business but never interfere in it,' she told him, taking another piece of toast.

'Hannah, do you know Lady Olivia well?'

'As well as anyone really knows her outside the inner circle up at the Park and maybe old Miss Plumm. Lady Olivia, whether you know her or not, always leaves her mark on you.'

'Even you and Jethroe, Hannah?' he asked.

'We're no exception. Jethroe was in love with Lady Olivia. I think he still is and always will be. He'd lay down his life for her.'

'Why? And would you?' asked Harry, clearly intrigued by this information.

'If Jethroe even knew we were talking about her and our intimate affairs, he'd beat me within an inch of my life,' said Hannah, who'd turned beetroot red and looked frightened.

'I'll never tell him.'

She sat quite silent for several minutes. Harry thought then that he had lost her, that she was too frightened to give up any more secrets. Then she surprised him by beginning to speak in a more considered manner about herself, Jethroe and Lady Olivia.

'I'd never met anyone like her before. She was marked by beauty and passion, hotter than the sun. She could melt people's hearts and enjoy doing it. I had no idea that women could enjoy sex with both men and women, that women could love women – until I met her. Lady Olivia was a woman who knew how to love with courage. It was she who taught me how to give myself totally to sex and love, only I could never master being totally submissive to the man I love yet keep my own counsel, the way she could.

'I will never leave Jethroe. I have learned to accept him with the faults he has and don't think myself a lesser person for that. Maybe greater. We are and are not what we are. Lady Olivia is the beautiful adventurer we all yearn to be. We cherish her as we would cherish ourselves. She has changed so many of us here in the village but we've added nothing to her life. It was already whole and complete the way we want ours to be but can never quite achieve it. You see, none of us has the courage to take that last step over the edge, the way she does.'

'And Jethroe? What is their relationship?'

'Sexual, passionate. He's submitted to her in every-thing she's asked. It's because of her that he loves me with a new kind of passion now. She taught him how to make love to me adoringly. I owe her my happiness because she taught me that if I want to get past the brute in Jethroe that's my business, but the day he is no longer giving me what I want, I am whole and able to walk away without a backward glance.'

'You do understand she is most probably guilty of murdering the prince, Hannah?'

'Yes.'

'And must be caught and brought to justice?'

'No.'

'But how can you say that?'

'You don't know Lady Olivia. If she killed the prince, she was driven to do it. She was with him a long time. They adored each other but he was a strange man and whenever he came here with her she seemed enslaved by him. Lady Olivia adored him as he did her. But he was crazily possessive. She made him so happy. He made her his world and thought he could keep her locked away for his eyes only. It was common knowledge that he never accomplished that. They say it made him even more difficult to handle. Lady Olivia got under his skin.'

'On the night the car was abandoned at Sefton Under Edge, were you with Jethroe?'

'No, I'd gone home to visit my mother. Jethroe sur-prised me around ten-thirty when I was still tending the bar by offering me that night and the next day off. He even had a taxi waiting to take me to my mother's.'

'Was that unusual?'

'Yes. But he can be very generous with me when he wants to be.'

'So you never saw or heard the car?'

'No.'

'Did you hear an aeroplane taking off from Sir James's airstrip?'

'If one did, I never heard it. And I would have because Sir James and his flying friends always circle the village.'

'I've told you more than I should have, but I know you won't let me down and tell Jethroe how much I've blabbed.'

'No, I won't tell, but I must strongly suggest to you that it is not good for your self-esteem to be pulled down by Jethroe, no matter how much you love him. You're not as strong as Lady Olivia nor, from what I can see, the games player she is. Thank you for being so frank with me.'

Harry went directly upstairs to the sitting-room and reported the information he had gained from Hannah which he thought relevant to the case. They now had more facts: that Jethroe and Hannah were absent from the village the night that Lady Olivia arrived in Sefton Under Edge. Jethroe was still in the frame as a possible accomplice to get her away, most especially so because he apparently adored her.

Jenny was to interview the vicar, the Reverend Edward Hardcastle, while Joe's first appointment was with the staff at Sefton Park and Harry's with Gerry and Cimmy Havelock. They left the pub separately, Harry in his car, the others on foot. Each of them had called in advance to arrange an appointment at Harry's insistence. Joe would have been happier catching people off guard. When asked about possibly gaining the advantage by surprise, Harry told his assistants, 'I prefer them to be concerned about having to be interviewed by New Scotland Yard. A night of anxiety to put them on edge about some stranger delving into their lives and secrets.'

The small eighteenth-century stone church and yard were set on a hillock just above the village with a view of the duck pond, the pub being nearly on the edge of the village in one direction and the road leading to Sefton Park the other. There was something of the *beau idéal* about the scene, made even more so by the ancient yews in and around the area. Jenny Sullivan knew she was witnessing a scene of the highest type of excellence and beauty, such as she had never before experienced. When she reached the door of the church she turned round to view Sefton Under Edge. A sense of perfection, something special, stirred her emotions and brought tears to her eyes. She simply could not understand why this place had taken such a grip on her.

She heard the church door open but made no effort to see who stood behind her. The scene before her was too idyllic and she was trying to hold on to the moment for as long as she could. She felt she was experiencing a taste of heaven on earth. It vanished when the vicar placed his hand on her shoulder.

'A place kissed by the angels, don't you think?' he observed.

'You know, Reverend Hardcastle, I do think that. I

feel very privileged to be here.'

'So do we all, my dear. That's why we try never to abuse it.'

She put out her hand and shook the vicar's, introducing herself. Jenny was surprised to feel a tremor in his fingertips. He looked quite handsome and she sensed he was a good soul, as one would expect of a clergyman. Yet he seemed unable to look her directly in the eye. His were always shifting. Jenny sensed that he was not at all at ease about being interviewed. He offered her a tour of the building and a stroll through the church yard where she might view the ancient headstones. Jenny declined his invitation, saying that she would like a tour one day but for the moment must get on with her investigation.

The sun was bright and hot even at that early hour of the morning and Jenny suggested they should carry on their interview sitting on an old stone bench overlooking the village. She sensed she was at the right time, in the right place, and was certain of it when he suggested they should go to the vicarage instead and let his wife make them tea. When she declined he offered her tea at Miss Marble's. He even suggested coffee at the pub. It was clear he was frightened of being interviewed alone. Jenny was too good a detective not to realise she had him where she wanted him and would certainly keep him that way.

She began her interrogation of Edward Hardcastle with the usual questions about himself and his family: how long he had been vicar of Sefton Under Edge, the lifestyle of the community, the behaviour of its residents.

The more questions she asked, the more personal they became and the more nervous he seemed to be. They did, however, have some empathy with one another. The vicar sensed the detective was trying to do her job with as much discretion as possible, while Jenny sensed from his answers and his manner that he was not trying in any way to hinder her. The longer the interview lasted, the more sure she became that he was leaning on her for support in some way. The vicar was hiding a secret, she was sure of that, and though she wanted to learn it, she felt sorry that it was going to be at his expense.

Jenny, having at last run out of the mundane questions so necessary to any investigation, prepared herself to deliver her *coup de grâce*. She sat silently for several seconds then rose from the bench and paced back and forth in front of Hardcastle, abruptly stopping short before him.

'Are you hiding Lady Olivia, Reverend Hardcastle?' she asked.

Her voice had changed now, all softness gone. Her question took Edward Hardcastle by surprise. He visibly paled. 'No,' he stammered.

'Is anyone else in the village keeping her in hiding?' she asked with that same steely edge to her voice.

'Not to my knowledge. And if they were I'd know about it,' he answered.

'I'm sorry to upset you with these questions about Lady Olivia as clearly I am,' she told him in a softer, more friendly voice as she sat down beside him once more.

'Much as I would like that not to be the case, I'm

afraid it is. You can't imagine how much her disappearance is upsetting everyone in the village and at the Park,' he told her, a tremor of emotion in his voice.

The vicar was breaking down, just as Jenny had hoped he would do. Now she withheld all mercy and went after him in honeyed tones. 'How well did you know Lady Olivia?'

'Well, Detective Sullivan,' he replied.

'Days, weeks, months, years? Casually, intimately?' Jenny pressed him.

'I believe this interview to be an invasion of my privacy,' said the vicar, and rose from the bench.

'Please sit down. You must answer my questions whether you believe them to be an invasion of your private life or not. If you care for Lady Olivia, you should confide all that you know about her and her whereabouts to me. Even any thoughts on where she might be. The more information I can gather about her to obtain a true picture of her, the better the chance we have of finding her. And, believe me, that we must do if there is to be any hope of clearing her name. Surely that is what you want?'

'You simply do not understand what torture this scandal and the disappearance of Olivia is for the friends who love her. Of course we want her name cleared and for her to come home but that isn't going to happen, is it?'

'Then you believe she's guilty of murder?'

'I didn't say that. What I am saying is you will have to clear her name *in absentia* for she is gone from us forever. It's a tragedy for her that she will be hunted all her life, and for us that we will never see her again.'

'We will find her, you know. One way or the other.'

'What does that mean?' asked the vicar in a voice that was barely a whisper.

'Dead or alive,' she answered.

With that he rose from the bench and walked away from the detective. He took no more than a couple of steps before he turned around and, walking back to Jenny, said, 'You must, I realise, do your duty but I wish that you had known Olivia then you would understand what a special young woman she is. You would see that she could not have done such a thing as to take another's life unless she was fighting for her own. And, knowing her, you would not hound her so ruthlessly. Is the life she must now lead – alone, dead to all she loved – not punishment enough? If you would stop chasing her down like a wild animal, she might find the courage and the time to repent her misdeeds and get on with a new life.'

The vicar was trembling, on the verge of breaking down. Jenny rose from the bench and led him back to it. They sat down together. 'You were in love with her,' said the astonished detective.

He slumped over and placed his head in his hands. He wanted to weep but the tears would not come. He had been carrying his love for Olivia in the dark recesses of his soul. Had kept his guilty secret and been conducting a fantasy sexual affair with her for so many years it was now a part of his life. At last someone recognised his passion for Olivia. It was very nearly a miracle that Jenny's words should unchain his secret. She had set him free to face his love for Olivia.

'Why don't you tell me about it? Maybe then I can learn what she's really like and will be better able to help her,' Jenny cajoled.

'I've known her ever since I took over this parish. She was always an enchantress even as a little girl. Year after year as she grew up we waited for her to lose her beauty and charm to adolescence, in young womanhood to gain a more sober approach to life. It never happened. She was well brought up like the Buchanan girls, her best friends, but there was about her something untamed, a wild and fearless nature that drove her always to live on the edge, to take that little step further. She was a friend to my children, always in and out of our house. She has a very good mind and often challenged me theologically. She knew how to stir my blood. On her eighteenth birthday ball at Sefton Park, a glamorous affair with hundreds of guests including all the village, young and old alike, she outshone every person present. There wasn't a man in the ballroom who did not lust after her. I was just one of them. She had seduced me years before and I had not realised it.

'It was so natural for her to make men feel wonderful, so irresistible. She made love to you with her flattering, teasing, challenging ways. I hungered for her, wanted a taste of her, to hold in my heart and soul forever. She felt something special for me and let me know it in a hundred different ways and as often as she could. I was tantalised by the richness of her spirit and wanted it to rub off on me. Time and again she taunted me with her sexuality, not as a tease but because she knew how much

I wanted her without the courage to take her from fear of scandal, love for my wife and family, and most of all deference to God and all I believed in.

'My fantasy sexual life with Olivia turned into an obsession. There wasn't a day went by that I did not live a portion of it in lust with her. All in my mind. You see, I never touched her. I never told her how I felt about her. Thoughts of sex, some of it depraved, were taking over my life. We would go on long walks together along the banks of the trout stream, ostensibly talking theology. But all the time in my mind I was fantasising about sex with Olivia. It was the same for her too though she never spoke to me about it. She showed me in the way she would touch my hand or sometimes kiss it, stroke my cheek, rub her body against mine. Once she ran her finger across my lips and I very nearly swooned with the thrill of her touch. I was tortured with love for her.

'One day she saw my pain and said the only intimate words that ever passed between us. "Edward – love, passion, sex – for me they are transient things, wonderful games so long as my partner knows they are fun and only one side can be the winner. I never play with a man if it's going to shoot arrows into his heart and leave him to bleed to death. It's always hard to leave someone you love but we must part because you love me too much." '

Jenny had to clear her throat before she could reply. 'You still love her!'

'How can I not? No other human being or belief, with the possible exception of my faith, has given me more, set me free as Olivia has. Who has been more honest and loving towards me, asking for nothing without making demands? Would that she had come to me that night for help! I don't know what I would have done but it would never have been to trap her into something she knew she could not do: turn herself in. My heart is sore to think of her alone somewhere in the world, having to reinvent herself to save her life. I pray that God will protect her. I think it somewhat pathetic that that is all I can do for someone who has given me so much pleasure and asked for nothing in return. What you have to know, Detective Sullivan, is that she is a giver, she is love, even if she is maybe a murderer. But we will never know that for sure. She has left us free to believe whatever we choose to believe. She fled the scene of that crime because she believed it was the right thing for her to do, for her own self-preservation and for her friends' peace of mind. She simply could not bend to the scandal.

'I can tell you one more thing about Olivia. She would never have stooped so low as you have to get me to break down and confess. And now, would you like to visit our church?' asked the Reverend Hardcastle.

Jenny Sullivan had never before been made to feel as low as she did at that moment. She felt as dirty as if she had crawled through mud to win his painful confession.

Chapter 8

September and Angelica were as close as two sisters could be. They thought of Olivia as part of their extended family, almost a sister. Angelica was four years older than September, a year younger than Olivia. September and Olivia had always been goddesses in her eyes and James a god. The three women and James confided in one another and when Marguerite came on the scene as lover to James she too had soon become a part of their lives, an intimate friend.

There was something vaguely incestuous about their closeness that was apparent to their wide circle of friends. Not that anyone believed for a minute that James slept with his sisters. It was more the demonstrative way they behaved when together. They had all had long-term as well as brief relationships. They had even swapped partners with ease, excited by the threesomes and group sex that took place when lust led them into sexual game playing. In their intimate group, love and sex were transitory pleasures. It had been Olivia who had made them understand the beauty and the thrill of untrammelled sex and how to keep it uncomplicated.

They were dazzling, thrilling, fun people. Intelligent, bright and amusing, with enough style and class to know how never to be vulgar and flaunt their sexual freedom and preferences in public. For that reason they had an intriguing reputation which was gossiped about but never proved.

The Buchanans worked hard and played hard. Each of them an achiever and all successful. Marguerite was a media star; Olivia was brilliant at anything she wanted to be, but passion and love were her greatest achievements. She had always been the teacher, the leader of her friends. September, a dedicated and successful painter, had the eye of the critics and the support of several museums. Angelica was a young surgeon of great promise. And their brother James, who ran the estate, was a famed lepidopterist with discoveries of several rare butterflies to his credit. Their work and achievements made them fascinating people to be with. They all worked very hard on their lives and their souls.

September hardly slept after she'd walked away from Harry. All night long she tried to work out in her mind what was happening to her. It was something fundamental, so strong and so right that she no longer felt like the same person. She felt herself to be something more than she had been when she'd held out her hand to him and he had swung himself behind her on her horse. Was it possible that real and true love could instantly turn your life around? Olivia would have approved of their falling in love. Had it not been she who had said that she was always in love, and happy to submit totally to her man of the moment in the name of that love? That was, so

116

long as she was able to keep her own counsel. Once that was denied her the romance was over.

Olivia had loved James that way but they could not sustain their love. The break-up had been no one's fault. Being apart allowed them still to love one another, even occasionally have sex together.

The prince had brought about fundamental changes in Olivia. Thinking about it, September believed that Olivia had found her real and true love just as she had recognised hers in Harry. The tragedy of Olivia and her prince was that he was a rotter who found a jewel of a woman and wanted to enslave rather than appreciate her. Olivia was real true love personified. The prince was real true depravity.

September's first loyalty had to be to her friend. Harry would understand that, she was certain. After an agonising night September decided that whatever happened with Olivia she would stand by her but to give Harry up was an impossibility. She had asked him to let Olivia go, he had declined and that would have to be the end of it. There was nothing to be done but to take their love affair a day at a time. Fate had declared she would be agonising over one or the other of them for the rest of her life.

September telephoned Angelica in her Oxford rooms but there was no answer. A message left on the machine informed her that her sister would be at Sefton Park in time for lunch. September felt a wave of relief wash over her. To be with her was better than discussing on the telephone how love for Harry was changing her life.

★ ★ ★

Angelica was in bed with her lover Neville Brett when the silence and darkness of the room was broken by the sound of the telephone and then September's voice on the answer machine. It meant nothing to the lovers who were lost in a sexual landscape so beautiful and exciting it was impossible for them to be distracted by the outside world.

Angelica and Neville had been carrying on a clandestine affair for more than two years. They were extremely happy with the arrangement they had with one another until six months before when Marguerite had come into their lives in more than a casual way.

Neville, a Harley Street consultant with an international reputation for excellence, was a tall, broad-shouldered man who had more the look of an athlete than a surgeon with his silver-grey hair which he wore on the long side, his dark brown eyes, a square face that was large and interesting, pronounced cheek bones and a handsome Roman nose. He was something special. No one could quite label what made him that way. It was more a combination of things. His appearance of powerful masculinity, his warm, gentle but firm manner, his sense of humour and remarkable ability with the scalpel added up to excellence as a surgeon and a compassionate human being.

Neville was the sort of man who knew how to put his life and career together, how to make his family work if not his marriage. At the time he met Angelica he was still happily married with four children. His wife was not. For all the years of their married life he had mistakenly believed that she loved him. He had never been unfaithful to her until he met three women visiting one of his patients. The patient was a Saudi prince and the three women were Marguerite, Olivia and Angelica.

The charm and vivacity these women exuded was something he had never experienced before. They were formidable females, hard to resist for their beauty, intelligence and sensuality. He spent no more than fifteen minutes in their company and for the first time ever realised that he was a lonely man. That passion and love had eluded him because his wife, whom he'd thought possessed those things, simply withheld them from him.

They had married when they were young and had their children straight away. She had chased after Neville until she caught him. It was one of those marriages where they went through hard times, poverty, his rarely having time for her and their children while he built his career. She had been happy then, running his life and their family. It was when things got better and the accolades from his peers and patients kept coming, and money was no longer a problem, that his wife became unhappy. She was always competing with him, treating him with little more than disdain. In public and private always trying to control him. He was not bothered by her behaviour, never spoke to her about it except merely to suggest to her that her obsession with being in control was neither healthy nor good for any of the family. That because of her pathological need to control and her attention seeking, their life together had lost its lustre and most certainly love.

For days after he met the three women Neville could

not get them out of his mind. It excited him to remember those few minutes. As a result he walked with a quicker step, he smiled more, felt alive in a new and different way than he had ever felt before. The next time he made love with his wife he realised that she actually worked at not enjoying sex with him. Her orgasms seemed to come in spite of her holding back. Neville understood now that she resented giving him the passion and sex he wanted to share with her.

It took three beautiful ladies and their magical love and sensuality to show him how little his wife gave him. How she had controlled their marriage and their family and was constantly diminishing him to raise herself a little higher. Then, having seen it so clearly, he felt sadness for his wife because she would never be more than the wife of Mr Neville Brett, because that was all she wanted. It was enough for her but not enough for him. And so after considerable thought he took a sabbatical from her and his Harley Street practice and accepted a post as Director of Surgery at a hospital in Oxford.

He had been there for several months when, after a five-hour operation, exhausted and concerned for his patient, he was sitting in the ante-chamber to the operating theatre when another surgeon entered from an adjacent theatre and sat down next to him. Both were still in their greens: cap, mask, and gowns. Neville's mask was off, dangling round his neck. He reached down next to him and took a cigar from the box of Dunhill's Special Havana. Then, looking at the doctor sitting next to him, reached for the box, opened it and offered one. The surgeon removed the mask with one hand and pulled the cap off with another, revealing a head of short curly chestnut brown hair and a lovely face wearing a smile that warmed his heart. They both burst into laughter.

Neville closed the lid of the box and replaced it on the chair next to him. 'Well! You're a lovely surprise, and clearly not a smoker of Havana cigars,' he told Angelica, a smile of delight still on his face.

'No, but my brother is.'

Neville was enchanted by her. He retrieved the wooden box and, opening the lid once more, said, 'Then you must select one for him.'

Angelica made her selection and, placing it close to her ear, rolled it between her fingers, then sniffed it. 'That's very generous of you, Mr Brett. Come home with me this evening and smoke it with him.'

'That's extraordinarily kind of you, but I think I would rather take you out to dinner. You see, I have wondered about you and the other two women you were with when we met before. If you dine with me this evening you can satisfy my interest.'

They had dined that evening and a life of erotic wonder opened for them. A sexual love affair developed that both entered with their eyes open to the reality of their situation. Both Angelica and Neville accepted the difference in their ages, their passion for their work, his being a married man. They conducted their affair without illusions and kept their liaison as secret as possible without hurting their relationship, always keeping in mind that both of them deserved better than they were giving each other.

Neville wanted an exciting, beautiful, clever wife – all the things that Angelica was. But this generous, thrilling young woman had too much life to live and work to do before she was ready to be a wife. They loved their life together and each other too much to sacrifice all Angelica's dreams and ambitions. Theirs was an intense affair made more so by the fact that they knew that one day a very special woman who was not twenty-eight would come along and put an end to their stolen moments of exquisite bliss.

Now Neville was lying on his side, holding Angelica close in his arms, one of her legs draped over his hip. His thrusts were slow and deliberate, deep, bringing her enormous pleasure. They kissed: lips, nipples. His hands and mouth ravaged her. She moaned with pleasure.

He held back his own pleasure until she had come several times and finally allowed himself the luxury of yet another orgasm. When they came together and she felt the warmth of his life's force flowing into her, she clung on to his phallus, gripped it tight with her cunt, made love to him with it. Her passion overflowed and she kept coming in orgasms one after the other, giving, giving herself totally to him.

Neville could feel his heart racing, his passion for such perfect sex with Angelica at that moment taking over his life. He was experiencing perfect bliss. So overwhelmed was he by his lust, by the sheer joy he discovered in all things erotic and love with a woman wanting to give, to please, submit to her man and derive exquisite bliss for herself in doing so, that tears were rolling from the corners of his eyes.

Angelica licked the salty teardrops from his cheeks and crawled into his arms. Entwined they fell asleep.

Harry arrived at Sefton Park just before eleven o'clock for his appointment with Sir James. But first he asked Fever if he could speak to September. He simply couldn't lose her. The aged butler told him she was not at home but had left a message for him. Fever handed him an envelope and Harry was ushered by the butler into the library. Once alone there he opened the envelope and read:

> The wolf also shall dwell with the lamb,
> and the leopard shall lie down with the kid.

Harry closed his eyes for several seconds and took deep breaths. He had not realised how fearful he had been that she was lost to him forever. Opening his eyes, he read the lines aloud to the empty room. How clever she was to have chosen them from the Old Testament. They said it all without saying too much or too little. She made no commitment but insinuated, 'It's all still possible for us.' He knew in his heart, as he was certain she did, that there was hope for them. He placed the note in the inside pocket of his jacket where it lay close to his heart. How clever and honest she was. He loved her all the more.

James entered the library followed by Fever who tottered in carrying a large and heavy French baroque silver tray laden with a coffee service, cups, saucers and plates, none of which matched. It was nevertheless the finest porcelain, bits of Limoges, Sèvres, Haviland, the last of the family's dinner, tea and coffee services. A Lalique pedestal dish proffered a pyramid of chocolate oatmeal biscuits made by Mrs Much. The old butler's hands shook dangerously while the china trembled and slid around on the tray. Harry very nearly sighed with relief when the tray was finally placed on one of the library tables. He was amazed to see everything still intact on the tray rather than on the floor.

James poured the coffee. While handing a cup and saucer to Harry, he said, 'Fever has run this house for more than sixty-five years. One learns to ignore certain aspects of his performance. It is after all only right since he turns a blind eye to our lifestyle. He is the oldest member of this household. I thought you bore up very well and appreciate the way you didn't offer to relieve him of his burden. He would have been mortified.'

Harry noticed the twinkle in James's eye and the faint smile on his lips. There was an atmosphere in Sefton Park of gentle, eccentric elegance that arises only from centuries of breeding and proud possession. The place was the last word in shabby chic, full of aged, knocked about family heirlooms. (The Buchanans never sold anything.) Harry felt comfortable in the library since his own rooms at Albany were in much the same style. But how would James know that? It amused him to think that the baronet probably pictured the policeman in a two up and two down in Croydon, in which Harry probably would be living on his detective's pay if not for his uncle's legacy.

'Help yourself to the biscuits, Detective Chief Inspector. I understand from Marguerite that you have a liking for sweets.'

'Are there no secrets in Sefton Under Edge? Does Marguerite tell you everything?'

'She has done about your meeting with her yesterday. This is a most unpleasant affair. We're all very upset about Olivia and what has happened. Concerned that she is all right wherever she is. You've erupted into our lives and we're frightened of you because you're delving into them and using us to help you catch someone we love very much.'

Harry could see that James was genuinely upset. The two men sat down round a library table littered with large leatherbound books, some open, some closed, and a very old portable Olivetti typewriter sitting in its canvas travelling case which was unzipped.

'Why don't we start this interview by my telling you what I already know about you, Sir James?'

'James will do,' he answered.

For some reason his casual manner, suggesting he be addressed on first-name terms, took Harry off guard. Did James know about September and his visitor? That relationship could not be allowed to have any bearing on his official enquiry. Harry had wanted James to be the more vulnerable of the two, it would have made his job easier. But that was never going to happen. He sensed that the other man's strength and intelligence was at least as keen as his own. Immediately he understood that he would have to approach James, who after all was just as much a suspect as anyone, quite directly if he expected to learn anything about what had happened to Lady Olivia after she arrived at Sefton Under Edge.

'I believe you are Sir Belville James Charles Edward Buchanan, baronet. Is that correct?'

'Yes.'

'You are thirty-two years old and single, have never been married?'

'That is correct.'

'You have an Oxford doctorate in Lepidoptera, are an authority on butterflies and have discovered several rare species that have been named after you. You travel on expeditions to rain forests around the world while working. You also own and run this estate successfully. You are considered one of the most interesting and sought after men in England. Although you are reclusive, periodically you are drawn into society. Your door is always open to your friends. You are an excellent pilot and collect vintage aircraft. You have a private grass airstrip.

'Now the problem I have with all this data on you is that it comes straight out of *Who's Who* or *Debrett's* and tells me nothing about the private man. I want to understand your relationship with Lady Olivia Cinders so that I can deduce whether you aided and abetted her escape from England by flying her across the Channel.'

James looked pained. 'I really resent your invasion of our privacy here at Sefton Under Edge, Chief Inspector. Your presence has put everyone on edge, made us take a good look at ourselves and re-examine our passion for Olivia. This is a village where nothing untoward ever happens. Suddenly a car is abandoned, Olivia creates a scandal and vanishes, and as a result our lives are closely scrutinised by a man from New Scotland Yard. Unless you can conceal your presence here from the media we shall soon be swamped by a merciless horde and will have yet another intrusion to resent,' said James matter-of-factly.

'That's why I must work quickly and I need your co-operation. James, you can't get out of it. Wherever I turn in this investigation, Olivia's friends have closed ranks to thwart me. Not one of you has come to terms with the fact that she is a murderess – she has taken a man's life and run away. Not one of you has considered yourself to be in a moral dilemma. And you are all arrogant enough to tell me that if she had come to you, you would have helped her to flee from justice. Can I not appeal, if not to your sense of justice, to your adoration of Lady Olivia? For her sake, please co-operate with me to discover the truth and let me move forward from here.'

James rose from his chair and went to stand by the window, looking across the gardens and the rolling fields beyond, seeing the ruined Tudor remnants of his ancestors' great house. Now he was being asked to leave this haven of privilege, this enclosed world, to face real life and deal with it on someone else's terms.

'Everyone lives two lives simultaneously: a public and a private one. It's in our private life that we confront our most intimate natures, our fantasies, the real truth about who and what we are. It is in our private lives, our seclusion from the outside world, that we are at our purest and live in truth. That is where we are whole and without artifice. You are an invader, Harry, and when you are done with us you will have ruined our privacy, infringed on our secret souls. Our lives will change after you have gone but we will not be able to blame you because it had already begun the moment Olivia slit the prince's wrists. So let's get on with this.

'Did I have anything to do with aiding her escape? No. Would I have helped if she had asked me to? Yes, without hesitation, and never given it another thought. Did I see her that night? No. Has she been in touch with me since that night? No. Now what more than that do you want to know that is relevant to Olivia's disappearance?'

James had virtually taken over the interview. It had been simple; he cut to the real issues, declared them then furnished the answers. Clever. A lesser detective might have been satisfied with his performance but Harry was not. What James had volunteered might or might not be true. He had been at ease until he played that volunteer question and answer game. Now he seemed sadder, upset even.

Harry jumped in. 'Everything and anything I can find out about Lady Olivia and that night could be relevant to my investigation. And so may I continue with my interview? *I'll* ask the questions and *you* furnish the answers.'

'Point taken, Detective Chief Inspector.'

'I would appreciate candid answers, and I would like to assure you that I intend to keep all the interviews I conduct here at the Park and in Sefton Under Edge confidential.'

'Your word as a gentleman?' asked James.

'If you like.'

'Then let's get on with it,' was the reply.

'What were you doing on the evening in question, the night of the murder?'

'I gave a dinner that turned into rather a late affair where everyone drank too much and talked long into the night on the influence of Byron on Delecroix. Then sex reared its delicious head. I see no need to elaborate any further about that.'

Harry then asked who had been at the party and was disappointed to learn that all his chief suspects had been there: Marguerite Chen, the three Buchanans, a lover of Marguerite's, and another of Angelica's who'd arrived late in the evening with a rather famous sculptor who was swept away to September's studio. The house party could substantiate each other's alibis.

Harry now had to decide whether all the party guests had colluded in helping Olivia's escape and deliberately arranged to furnish each other with rock solid alibis: a united front to conceal a common cause. Now he would have to look to the servants and the estate workers for clues with which to break his suspects' alibis.

'No need for any further detail at the moment,' he confirmed, keeping control of the interview. 'How many planes are usually kept in the hangar on the edge of the airstrip?'

'Five.'

'Are they all still there?'

'So far as I know.'

'Why don't we walk over there and check and see?' suggested Harry.

'If you like,' said James.

Harry was impressed by what he saw when they reached the hangar. James pressed a button and the huge metal doors slid open one after the other to reveal a most handsome collection of bi-planes in perfect condition, looking rather like prehistoric butterflies. There was no reason to check whether one of them had a depleted petrol tank; too much time had passed in which it could have been refilled. One dead end seemed to follow another in all the paths Harry raced down in pursuit of the killer. He had that rare thing, for him at least, a premonition of defeat. The killer had got away. He shook it off as the two men left the hangar.

'Could a plane have taken off from this field on the night in question, James?' asked Harry.

'Yes, quite easily. There are sunken runway lights. A flip of a switch in the offices at the field or the library in the house and the strip is ready for night take off or landing. But Olivia could not have taken off from here. You can see those lights for miles around. From the house clearly, from the village a bright glow. Someone would have seen or indeed heard a plane that night.'

'That's what I'm here to ascertain.'

Walking back across the fields towards the house, James volunteered out of the blue, 'Olivia is a constant worry to me. You don't know her and can't imagine . . . to know her is to live at the top of one's life, where the air is thinner, more refined. The very idea of never seeing her again makes me feel wretched, as if I have been robbed of a portion of my life. Try and understand – she is something very special, a woman brave as a man, courageous as a tiger, clever as a fox, sly and insinuating as a panther. And for all that one of the sexiest women I have ever met. She loves sex, lives in a world of eroticism that she wants to share with everyone. She is a sensual adventuress and wants all her most intimate friends to enjoy the same highs and lows of boundless sex as she does.'

'You're in love with her!' exclaimed Harry.

'Madly, passionately. For every moment of every day. She lives and loves in perfect freedom, knows how to take the real world on the tip of her finger and spin it. She makes the heart beat faster. No, that is too trite. Instead she teaches one how important it is to make the heart beat faster, let passion fly, above all to love in the grand manner.

'That's why September asked you to let Olivia go. Why I ask you now, and Angelica will in her turn. Have you any idea how much it pains us that she did not come to us so we could help her? We were her lovers, her play-mates, her friends, and she loved all of us and made us a part of her life.

'Every human being has the capacity to murder if provoked. Olivia has always had that dark side to her nature. She has played with it and sometimes taken us with her. For a game. She always felt sure that she could beat the devil. Then the prince came along and she fell under his spell and then in love with him. He was able to play sexual games with her that became ever more dangerous. He was passionately in love with her, as we all have been, but it was he and his dark soul who took her over, enslaved her in their intimate life. We saw her change over the years she was with him, drift farther and farther away from us, returning only periodically to remind us how much we loved her.

'Harry, that is the woman you so eagerly want to know about because you think that by doing so you will be able to pre-empt her movements. It will never happen. You will never be sitting under a palm tree, waiting for her to step off a yacht, or at an airport in some remote country, ready to cuff her when she descends from a plane.

'I don't know why she left the car here. That is just as much a mystery to me as her being able to vanish so completely and slip the world-wide net you have thrown to catch her.'

Chapter 9

When Harry and James arrived at the front entrance to Sefton Park Harry did not enter the house. Instead he told James, 'Thank you for being so candid with me. There's nothing more I want to ask you at this time.'

The two men shook hands and James asked him, 'Since you are due back here to interview September later in the day, would you like to stay for lunch? Angelica will be here and I'm sure you will want to question her too.'

Why was he being so hospitable? Why, in fact, had he been so forthcoming about the intimate lives of the Buchanans and Lady Olivia? Had it all been genuine or merely a clever ploy to make Harry believe none of them had seen her on the night in question nor heard from her since? Harry tended to believe that James was telling the truth and the only reason to question September and Angelica was to corroborate his story. He felt sure they would bear out their brother's account. But what had been James's reason for giving such a detailed profile of Lady Olivia, showing both the light and dark side of her nature? What exactly was James trying to say – that he knew her capable of killing the prince but that she should still be left free to salvage her own soul, mete out her own punishment? And, not least of all, had James opened his heart to draw a picture of Lady Olivia that Harry would find irresistible?

Harry declined the invitation and, much to James's surprise, asked him to tell September that he would not be questioning her after lunch as planned, but would call her to arrange another appointment. James walked him to his car and waited until Harry was out of sight before returning to the house.

It was a relief for him to get away from Sefton Park. The interview with James had helped convince him that no one in that house had seen or helped Lady Olivia's getaway. He contemplated that fact all the way back to The Fox. Then as he parked the car, cut the motor and pulled up the handbrake, Harry hit the steering wheel with the open palm of his hand and said aloud, 'You were good, James, very good, but not good enough. Every suspect will be interviewed, redundant or not.'

When he entered the pub his eyes immediately settled on the landlord. Jethroe Wiley had yet to satisfy Harry that he was not a suspect, and who was the man the postman had seen in the early hours of the morning, wearing Jethroe's cap and jacket and accompanied by his gun dogs? Harry ordered a platter of assorted sandwiches and lager, three chocolate mousse puddings and coffee to follow then took the stairs to the ops room two at a time.

Joe was still out but Jenny was there. Her first words

to Harry were, 'The sooner we get out of this so-called paradise the better.'

'Why's that?' he asked, sitting on the end of the table at which she was working.

'I don't exactly know why but there's something so cloyingly perfect about the place, so storybook ideal, it undermines all that I am and stand for. The vicar actually told me that he considered Lady Olivia – a murderess! – more honourable and deserving than I am. That I, by contrast, had behaved deviously in order to get him to confess his very intimate feelings for her. It feels as if, wherever she is, Lady Olivia is still a powerful presence for everyone I speak to. She's far too clever, a woman who has everything and knows how to use it without even trying. The vicar made me feel dishonest. She makes me feel insignificant, as a woman and as a detective.'

'You're hardly that! You're a very promising young detective who might one day be a great one. You have no need to feel insecure. Stop measuring yourself against Lady Olivia. I've learned a great deal about her. She's a natural seductress of both men and women, whether present or not. You'll have to learn how to handle that, not be intimidated by her. Now, what did you learn from the vicar?'

Jenny felt much better after her pep talk from Harry. She flipped through some pages of notes and reported what she had learned from the vicar. Harry was impressed. She had got Hardcastle to reveal his deepest, darkest secret. Harry went to the blackboard standing on an easel in the corner of the room. He rubbed out the vicar's name and commented, 'There's something very peculiar about this case. There are almost too many suspects and no positive leads as to who helped our murderer to get away.'

He was still pondering that when the telephone rang. It was Jethroe announcing that Gerry Havelock was there, wanting to see Detective Chief Inspector Graves-Jones. Harry told the publican to tell Mr Havelock to take a table and that he would be down as soon as possible. Joe arrived at that minute followed by one of the waitresses bearing a wooden tray laden with their lunch and Jethroe with a second tray of glasses, plates, and a large bowl of crispy chips that Harry had not ordered. 'Just out of the fryer, a little treat on the house. A working lunch! When I was in the force I can hardly remember having any other kind,' he said as he disappeared down the stairs.

By now Harry disliked Jethroe Wiley who had all the characteristics that rubbed him up the wrong way. He was overfriendly, bombastic and frequently intrusive. He was too sure of himself by half, almost condescending towards Harry and his team. It was that condescension that caused him to shoot out of his chair and catch Jethroe when he was halfway down the stairs.

'Did I forget something?' he asked.

'I hope not. I'd like to ask you a few questions this afternoon. Shall we say about half-past three in the bar?' Then before Jethroe could give his reply, Harry had turned away and was back in the ops room.

The fax machine was spewing out paper as he walked over to the table and picked up a ham and cheese sandwich and a glass of lager. Joe tore the fax from the machine. 'Now this is interesting, sir. Lady Olivia Cinders has been sighted on three different occasions in South Africa. Once at a private airfield on the outskirts of Cape Town, twice on a sixteen-square-mile ranch that's sealed off by electric fencing and patrolled by a small army of security guards. It's private property and no one is allowed in or out without the owner's permission. You're going to like *this*, sir – the owner is none other than Lady Olivia Cinders herself.'

'I want to know everything about that tract of land and I need to speak to the local police there. Not one of the people we've spoken to nor her solicitor has said a word about her owning such a property.'

'Is it possible that she never revealed the information to them?' queried Joe.

'Anything's possible, but I doubt it. I want to know how she got that property, and when. I want to know everything we can find out about it and to speak to the witnesses who saw her there. Get that together as soon as possible, Joe. I don't like it. It's too perfect in a case where nothing is going our way.'

'You think someone's playing cat and mouse with us, sir? But who would do that?'

'Who indeed? Her friends, perhaps? No, I doubt that. I've come to know Lady Olivia Cinders through this investigation and how she behaves with her friends, the way her heart and mind works. She would never draw them into such a scandal. Maybe out of desperation she did to obtain a car, but she would never use them deliberately to sow false leads. I suspect these sightings in South Africa may have been well planned and executed by her so that I will fly there to chase her down.

'If that should prove to be the case, she will have made her first mistake. She will have pointed up the possibility that the murder of the prince was premeditated, very well planned, even down to her escape. Only something went wrong: the prince's brother arrived on the scene. All this, of course, is supposition. That's why I need you to get me whatever information you can to verify this fax. Stay on it. What else have you got for me?'

'The staff at Sefton Park were very reticent over talking about Lady Olivia and the night in question. I got the usual paeans of praise of the lady. They're shocked by what has happened and by her running away. After I assured them she did indeed murder the prince, and in a most bizarre way, they were visibly upset. They're decent, simple people, long standing workers for the Buchanans. They spoke of Sir James and his sisters in glowing terms. Easy to work for, honest, a little eccentric but loyal to their workers and always fair.'

'Did they see anything out of the ordinary on the night in question?'

'Nothing. One of the farm-hands says he was surprised to see a light on in the hay barn at about two in the morning. He went to the barn and called out several times. There was no answer, so he switched off the light. In the morning, when he went back to the barn, he found a horse blanket. He thought no more than that someone had been playing hanky-panky in the barn, and returned the blanket to the stables.

'The house staff and the farm- and stable-lads all

knew the prince and Lady Olivia. In the last two years the pair of them spent a good deal of time there. They stabled a pair of horses at the Park because they were keen riders and enjoyed memberships of several hunts. The prince was extraordinarily generous to the house staff and the stable-lads, though intensely jealous if Lady Olivia even talked to anyone in his presence. It seems she was passionately in love with him, granted him his every wish, gave him all her attention. She seemed to change from the person she had always been, but they couldn't tell me exactly how. When she did arrive to stay at Sefton Park without the prince she reverted to being her old self: friendly, chatting with everyone. According to Mrs Much, the cook, they all felt the foreigner, meaning the prince, seemed to cast a spell on Lady Olivia.'

'I want that horse blanket and for you to cordon off the place where it was found. Call Chief Inspector Pike at Oxford and tell him to send forensic out here as soon as he can.'

The telephone rang and Harry answered it. 'I've been waiting for more than an hour for Detective Chief Inspector Graves-Jones – how much longer am I expected to cool my heels?' fumed an agitated Gerry Havelock.

'I'm so sorry, Mr Havelock, I shan't be much longer and I do apologise for keeping you,' said Harry, putting down the phone.

Turning to his associates, he said, 'Gerry Havelock is an arrogant man. Possibly sharp in business and a control freak, but far from wise. He's downstairs now because he was so defensive about being questioned about Lady Olivia before this that he walked out of the house after fifteen minutes and drove away. He called his wife and ordered her to summon their solicitor if she was asked any personal questions.'

'Hiding something,' commented Jenny.

'Now how do you figure that out?' asked Joe as he bit into a sausage and egg sandwich.

'Defensive, rude, and seeking us out because he knows he has made a bad impression. He'll want to win you over, sir, will try to explain his behaviour, and in order to do that he will have to tell you about that night and his relationship with Lady Olivia. He's harbouring a secret – one he doesn't want his wife to hear. He sounds the sort of man who'll feel obliged to clear his name to nurse his ego.'

'Not bad. Not bad at all, Sullivan,' said an admiring Joe.

Harry merely smiled at Jenny which she took for praise. 'Was Mrs Havelock at all helpful?' she asked.

'She's an innocent who copes with all her personal problems by ignoring them. A kind, gentle woman with a bastard of a husband who controls her. But besides the kindness and graciousness there's a backbone of steel. The only thing she had to say was that what had happened was a tragedy. That Lady Olivia had once been close to their family and loved by them all but that it was a long time ago. "She wouldn't come to us for help. We've been estranged from her for years except to say a brief hello. I can assure you she would never have approached any of my family for help."

'Those were her words. And I believe she was telling me what she believes to be the truth. As for whether it is . . . Well, I should know that after I interview her husband. By now he must be in a rage at being kept waiting so long. Just the way I want him to be,' said Harry as he rose from his chair and walked from the room.

About to descend the stairs, the telephone made him hesitate. 'If that's for me, I'll take it,' he announced.

It was and he returned to take the call. It was Marguerite Chen. 'Detective Chief Inspector Graves-Jones, will you and your associates come to dinner this evening? Shall we say eight o'clock? Good, see you then.'

He put the telephone down and he looked at his team. 'We've been summoned to dinner at Marguerite Chen's this evening. Now I wonder what that's all about?'

Things seemed to be turning themselves around. The suspects were now calling the investigators. There was no doubt in Harry's mind that Lady Olivia's disappearance from the lives of several people in Sefton Under Edge was having a shattering effect on them. In some strange way it was as if the murder of the prince had shaken the foundation of their lives. That *one of them* was capable of taking a man's life so easily, and could vanish into oblivion from a world they knew and loved, was a sobering experience.

Harry was beginning to understand the amoral stance they had taken out of loyalty to one of their own, a woman who had taught them how to love and be free. They had been taught by Lady Olivia to love themselves so they could love each other. One followed the other.

When September had asked Harry to 'let her go', she was saying just as much, 'Let me go, let all of us go to be responsible for our own crimes and punishments.' That élite inner circle must survive no matter what they had done, even at the expense of justice. But understanding their belief did not make it right. Not at least in Harry's eyes.

His heart ached for September, his body longed to be entwined with hers, but his search for Lady Olivia and justice was equally as important. Harry was a man who knew his priorities. He reminded Joe to get on with tracking down the South African information and walked down the stairs to meet Gerry Havelock.

There were only a few people left in the pub, more sitting outside in the sun. Jethroe was talking to Gerry. Both men fell silent as soon as they saw Harry.

'Mr Havelock, you wanted to see me?' were his first words.

There was a thunderous expression on Havelock's face. 'Shall we sit over there in the far corner? We'll not be disturbed,' he suggested.

'It's such a grand day – the sunshine and the warm breeze . . . why don't we walk down by the stream? I've yet to do that,' replied Harry, starting for the door. He could feel Havelock's irritation and didn't give a damn.

They hardly spoke to one another as they walked through the village and along the footpath by the stream. Gerry Havelock appeared to have calmed down somewhat by the time they arrived at a bench where he suggested they should sit. It was an ideal scene: the opulence of the woods on the other side of the stream, the sounds of birds singing happily in the trees. A fisherman in waders standing mid-stream and casting for an elusive blue trout. The scent of the undergrowth and a field of bluebells was a treat for Harry. It stirred his senses and he was once more aware of how special a place this was.

Gerry Havelock broke the silence. 'I should be in London, at a meeting in the city.'

'Then why are you not there, Mr Havelock?'

'Don't play coy with me, Chief Inspector! You know damned well why. After I stalked out of our meeting earlier, I thought my exit could be misconstrued. You might believe I dashed away because I aided and abetted Olivia in her escape.'

'Would you like to tell me why I might have thought that?'

'Because I couldn't bear to be questioned about her and this mess she has got herself into. I was rude and I fled. Your invasion of our privacy was bound to uncover deeply buried secrets I thought I'd never have to face again. Secrets that have left scars on me and my family, and all inflicted by Olivia.

'If she had come to Sefton Under Edge for help it would have been to me and no one else. I didn't want you to know that, nor did I want to talk to you about Olivia in my wife's presence. It took me and my family years to get over that particular relationship. We thought we were over her but still she remains under the surface of our skin, and I suppose she always will. I have sought you out because I want to make certain you believe me when I tell you neither I nor my family had anything to do with Olivia's escape.'

The men remained silent for a while. Gerry Havelock lowered his gaze and placed one hand on his forehead. Harry watched him for some minutes. Was it just the man's ego that demanded Harry should believe he was the only one to whom Olivia would have gone for help or was it true?

'Why should I believe you? Practically every person I have interviewed has said the same thing: she would have gone to them, but she didn't. If you want me to believe you, you will have to tell me why you and none of the others?'

'This is off the record, for your ears only and told to you because I want you to stop rooting about in the secret lives of the residents of Sefton Under Edge.

'I have a son called Raife. He fell in love with Olivia when they were in their early-teens. My wife Cimmy was charmed by Olivia, and mother and son saw to it that she spent a great deal of time with us. Olivia was addictive – one only needed a taste of her to crave more. Raife was hopelessly besotted with Olivia who could twist him round her little finger, while Cimmy thought she had found the daughter she'd never had and was besotted with her. She taught her to garden, Cimmy's passion, how to be charitable and work for the under-privileged. I was the father figure she'd never had, as well as the dashing, sophisticated, older man she craved. Soon she had us all playing the roles she wanted us to fill in her life.

'One day I drove her into London. There was such tension between us. I wanted her badly, as I had never wanted another woman. But she was not a woman, she was a tantalising young girl. Once on the outskirts of the city she slipped along the seat closer to me and ran her hand up the inside of my thigh. I thought I was going to explode with lust for her.

' "I'm in love with you, Gerry, have been for a very long time," she told me. "I think about sex with you constantly. I've seen that same look in your eyes. It's always there. I love Raife and Cimmy but I can't bear not to be made love to by you. I want you to take me somewhere where we can have sex, let our passion fly. Please don't tell me I've made a fool of myself." And tears came into her eyes.

'We found a small hotel where no one would know us. I have never known sex such as I had with Olivia. Her young flesh, her love of all things sexual to which I introduced her . . . we drove each other into a kind of erotic madness. After that first time in London neither of us could keep our hands off the other. We would have sex in the wood, in the garden, in my bed. It was always exciting and dangerous because Cimmy would be somewhere in the house, or Raife or both of them. We would have sex several times a week, anywhere we could find. In my office, for instance, with the door locked and my employees working outside. We longed to spend a night together and when we finally did Olivia wept because she felt guilty and confessed she had fallen in love with me. She wanted more of me than I could give her. She had begun having sex with my son in the hope he would be as thrilling a lover as his father. It was marvellous, she boasted to me, but still she wanted me, and the stable life that Cimmy had. She loved us as a family and had never meant to turn our lives upside down.

'The pain of loving me got to be too much for her and so Olivia walked out on me. I will never forget the look on her face when she told me, "You are an impossible love. I deserve better than that and so do you."

'We saw each other one more time. I told her I wanted to leave Cimmy for her but had not the courage, and could not bear the scandal. I begged her to give me time to ease out of my marriage. But by then she saw the way we felt for one another as tawdry and fled from me, from Raife, from Cimmy. A light went out of our lives. We each loved her in our own way. When Olivia fled from us and our lives fell to pieces we each came to understand what had happened. We had deceived each other, mother, father and son. Had been disloyal to everything we were to each other, and all for love of a young innocent girl.

'I never saw her alone again. I tried but she would never allow it. The hunger and love I felt for Olivia never went away. I know it was the same for her. She told me so once when I met her by accident in London. It was in an art gallery in the West End. She looked at me and sadness came into her eyes. "It was the best, our impossible love. It will never go away from me, no matter what time or distance is placed between us," she told me.

' "If ever you need me, for anything, promise you will come to me?" I told her then. She replied, "I would go to no one else." Then she walked away. So, you see, Detective Chief Inspector, that's how I know Olivia would have come to me. She would never have approached someone else.'

'And you never saw her or heard from her that night or at any time since the murder of the prince?' asked Harry.

'No! May I go now?' asked Gerry Havelock as he stood up, visibly upset by the memory of what he had lost.

Harry studied the distress on the man's face. He felt no pity for him but he did believe his story. 'Yes,' he said. And Gerry Havelock walked away, miserable, bereft, but confident of the love he had lost.

Harry sat on the bench for some time thinking about Olivia. What chance had she for a stable relationship with a man when she'd started off as a teenager with a bastard like Havelock? Had he resisted her, not taken her on and taught her the delights of sex, would she have turned out differently? It was an interesting question but unanswerable of course.

There seemed to have been a change in the course of the investigation. His suspects were more co-operative and yet not one of them had volunteered a single clue as to what had happened on the night of the murder that might help Harry to catch his quarry. It was quite extraordinary how this young and beautiful woman affected every person she touched, changed them in some way, set them free as they never could have been without her. She was theirs and they would never drive her from their hearts and minds. In just the short time Harry and his team had been in the village, turning the place and the people who lived there upside down with their questions, there'd been signs that they now accepted and believed that Lady Olivia was gone from their lives forever. With the gifts she had so generously given them, they were now striking out on their own to make richer lives for themselves.

Yes, Lady Olivia Cinders was indeed a fascinating, seductive creature. Harry doubled his resolve to find her and bring her to justice.

Chapter 10

Marguerite was standing by the window of her library, thinking about Olivia, her crime and disappearance. Olivia had always had a sense of self-worth that was awesome because it had not been contrived, she had never had to work on it. She was born with an innate love of self which was why it was so easy for her to love and leave people. She assumed all her friends were like her; when love and lust had run their course, they could always move on. It was the feminist's dream, true independence, utter non-dependence on a man to make her a valid woman.

Marguerite thought about herself, who and what she had made of her life, now, at the age of forty. A don at Oxford and an international media figure, an author writing scholarly books on American art of the twentieth century and its importance as a sociological phenomenon – not bad going for a lower-middle-class Chinese American girl whose great-great-grandfather had been a labourer on the first railroad crossing from the American mid-west to San Francisco.

All the generations of Chen women before her had

served as passive wives, slaves; the many aunts and cousins, nieces who worked for their families and their men, had lived in two worlds: the one their husbands and Chinese family demanded and the intimate relations they had with their female relations, their only social contact that enriched their lives.

It had been the Chen women who had scraped together the money to supplement the scholarships that Marguerite had won to attend Smith College in North-ampton, Massachusetts. Love and pride for Marguerite, who could speak for them, live out their fantasies of rising above their station, had given them a tremendous sense of self-worth. It had changed their lives. They owed each other a great deal.

Her father, a gruff, mostly silent man, found little he liked about his beautiful daughter. A man more indiffer-ent to her and her sisters and brothers than unkind, she loved him nevertheless; mostly because he was as kind and generous as he could be to the family, and he supported anyone who needed his help. The sadness was that he did not want his family to rise above themselves; he would only be happy with his children as long as they followed his footsteps as a fruit and produce seller in a small shop in San Francisco's Chinatown.

Marguerite walked from the window to look in the long narrow mirror framed in a sumptuous pattern of inlaid mother of pearl. It was Damascus work of the eighteenth century and purchased in the very city it was named after when lecturing there at the university for a semester.

She saw in the mirror a woman with a sharp, quick

intelligence to match her piquant, exotic looks. A lady with boundless energy, she was analysing herself because she was a woman who believed that people were not always what they seemed. That you must look deep into the soul really to know someone. Even yourself.

Marguerite ran her fingers through her silky black hair and was not displeased when she looked at herself objectively: chic but always subtle, an academic with gloss, impressive certainly. She liked the exotic quality about herself that enchanted people, and enjoyed her own charisma.

She walked back to the open window and sat on the sill, mind drifting back to that first time she and Olivia went to bed together. Too much champagne and cocaine for two women without inhibitions and who were overwhelmed with lust for one another. To this day Marguerite did not quite know how it happened, who was the aggressor or even if there was one. They had made love to each other. It had been thrilling to have sex with a woman. So different. A gentler kind of sex, the other woman's body as lovely as Venus. It had happened, it had been another sexual sensation, and Marguerite would not have missed it for the world. But they were not lesbians. Both women simply craved sex, erotic games, and preferred men to women as a rule.

Everyone in Sefton Under Edge and Sefton Park was changing now that Olivia was gone. Marguerite and the others had to come to terms with the fact that she had killed a man, her lover, for whatever reason, and might never be found. Marguerite had invited the detectives for dinner because she wanted to discuss the case with them, have it all out in the open and be done with the horror that had touched their lives.

She saw two figures walking across the park towards her house and recognised Neville Brett and Angelica. She waved to them. Her heart began to race and she felt warm and lustful. Seeing Neville always made her feel that way. For months she had been fighting her attraction to him. It was no secret they had feelings for each other. When in the same room they could hardly keep their hands off one another. They created that special kind of chemistry that exists in dreams but rarely with another human being.

They were in love with each other, the serious kind of in love that lasts for eternity. It had happened to them when Angelica brought him to Sefton Park for the first time. At first Marguerite thought it was only lust and tried to ignore it. But after half a dozen meetings with him she understood that she was in trouble. It was more than lust, it was a oneness she was feeling with him which she had never known with anyone before. She tried to run away from it. Marguerite even went to Angelica and told her she had a positively girlish crush on Neville.

Now, watching them walking arm in arm towards her, she remembered what Angelica had said. 'I adore him, Marguerite, we have a wonderful time with one another but we are not in love, that's the sadness of our relationship. We're best friends who like to have outrageous sex together. I see the way he looks at you, how he adores you from afar. One day we'll part and because we know that, I see other men, date them, bed them, and never talk about it to Neville. He does the same with other women and is enough of a gentleman to keep quiet about it. I think you should know that he's worth having a crush on but he will never stand for being made one of your transient lovers.'

That was what worried Marguerite. Neville Brett meant commitment, marriage, a life of togetherness, an erotic closeness she would never want to lose. In fact, she would fight to keep him. Her love for Neville made a mockery of all the things she had been preaching for the last twenty years, most of all her thesis that it was not necessary for a woman to be attached to a man for her to feel fulfilled and take her rightful place in society.

She had been to bed with Neville nearly six months ago. They had shared an erotic experience neither had wanted to end. For three days they hardly left her bed; when they did it was merely to eat or to walk in her rose garden. During their time together they gave themselves up to each other and fell very deeply into love.

It had been Marguerite who back-pedalled as fast as she could away from Neville after those three miraculous days. She moved on to what she knew she felt safe with: handsome young studs in awe of who and what she was.

She could see Neville and Angelica's faces quite clearly now. They waved at her as they approached the house. How handsome he looked, and how young and beautiful Angelica was. Marguerite's mind slipped back to the time after she and Neville had had their remark- able tryst. There had been flowers, so many flowers, with romantic cards telling her how much he loved her. His proposal of marriage was made over the telephone out of desperation because she would not see him. Marguerite rejected him, and instead of telling the truth, saying how much she loved him and wanted him for then and always, she gave him the same old rhetoric with which she had influenced and inspired women all over the world.

She well remembered how he had answered her; in fact she had a difficult time preventing those words from ringing in her head: 'You got it wrong, my dear. What you have been preaching has been brilliant for the unloved woman, the one who has to stand alone without the things she wants, and made those women strong and happy in their lives. But what about the millions of women who have found love with other human beings? They have no need to build walls around themselves and you forgot that. I'll wait, take your time. Do some fancy footwork and free yourself from your rhetoric. You don't have to live as you preached. You have a man who loves you now. Don't be afraid to experience that love.'

Her memories were interrupted by Angelica's voice. 'Hello. We've come to invite you to lunch. It seems like ages since I've seen you.'

Neville gazed into Marguerite's eyes and raised her hand to his lips. The magic between them was still there, Marguerite realised in confusion.

Angelica asked Neville to help her and stepped in through the window, to sit on the sill facing Marguerite. Neville watched these two women who had changed his life. His admiration for them and the manner in which they approached living, their accomplishments, sense of fun and generosity of spirit, had added a new dimension to his life. He wished that Olivia could be with them but he knew that that was an impossibility, they would never see her again. 'Any news?' he asked Marguerite.

'No. I suppose you've heard we're all being questioned by New Scotland Yard detectives? In fact, I've invited them to dinner tonight because I'm fed up with them snooping around and getting nowhere. I intend to ask them for the truth about what happened on the night Olivia allegedly murdered the prince, and then I think we should all be open and above board with them about her. How losing her is affecting all our lives, so that they will understand there is nothing for them here and go away and leave us to mourn the loss of our greatest friend. None of us will ever be the same without her.

'Will you come to dinner tonight? September and James are coming. It's going to be rather like laying a ghost. I think we should all be here so that once it's done we can get on with our lives.'

Angelica had gone pale. Neville took her hand and stroked it. She sighed. 'I know you're right, Marguerite. We have to have lives apart from Olivia. Of course we'll come. I think I'd like to go riding now.' And she slipped from the window sill to stand on the lawn next to Neville.

'I'll come along with you,' he offered.

'I'd rather ride alone, if you don't mind. Why don't you stay with Marguerite and both of you stop being so silly, wasting your lives apart from each other.

'Marguerite, if we're going to pick up our lives and do something with them, you two had better come to terms with love. We'll all be the better for it.'

She turned to Neville, slid into his arms and kissed him passionately on the lips. Then stepping away from him, she told him, 'I knew one day it was to be goodbye for us, my dearest lover-friend-mentor, but I did not know how or when it would happen. I suppose this is as good a time as any, and the way you and Marguerite love each other as good a reason. Let's skip lunch at the house. I'll see you here for dinner – the Buchanans in full strength.' And taking Marguerite's hand in hers, she smiled and squeezed it. Before they could say a word she was gone.

'Angelica constantly amazes me. It's always so easy for her to do the right thing at the right time. She's that way in the operating theatre as well, always totally focused, inspiringly swift and meticulous. She was born to be a great surgeon. I am so lucky to have met you all. I had forgotten how rich and exciting life and love can be,' Neville murmured.

Marguerite could find nothing to say in reply. She was too overwhelmed by what had just happened. She watched Neville pull himself through the window. A sense of oneness with him wrapped itself around her and she understood that life was giving her a second chance. She and Neville were two vigorous people who would not take from each other's lives, only add to them. They were successful, dedicated people in their work and neither would infringe on the other. Love would serve only to sustain their working lives. She was no longer the ambitious twenty-one-year-old who got burned by a hasty marriage to a lazy, macho vulgarian that ended five weeks after the wedding. The experience had turned her off marriage for good. Or so she had thought.

Only when she had met Neville had she realised she was tired of the young men who constantly came and went in her sexual life. Only with him did she at last see what she had missed by not marrying and having children. Fortunately Neville had been more clear-sighted and generous in waiting so patiently for her to come to her senses.

Now Marguerite threw herself into his arms and kissed him all over his face. He swept her up and carried her through the house and up to her bedroom.

There were no words to express the violent passion, the excitement of giving in to love and commitment. Two hearts that beat as one, bodies that felt as if they had been flayed. Wherever they were touched and kissed, licked and sucked, every nerve end was alive with lust. Thought vanished. Naked, they kissed each other's bodies, licked them, fondled them with hungry mouths, tongues, roving hands and fingers. Neville licked between her labia, sucked on them, nibbled them. While he made a feast of her cunt, she came and her copious orgasm was as nectar to him.

Marguerite lost control of herself and called out, howled her pleasure. She was in that place of no return. So deep in bliss she had to fight to stay alive. To die in orgasm was at the same time to live for a few seconds on another plane. Neville adored her in that state. He turned her round and put her on her knees to take her from behind in deep thrusts while he played with her breasts and tweaked her nipples, licking her back with his tongue. She came again – uncontrollable multiple

orgasms that took her breath away. She called out to
God between screams of bliss. Lust gone wild.

When Neville came he called out again and again,
thanking God for Marguerite. They collapsed on the bed,
entwined themselves in each other's arms. Marguerite
scooped their lust from her cunt as if it were a golden
vessel and together they licked from her palm and sucked
her fingers. This was more than nectar, it was the elixir of
life. They were born again, together and forever.

Harry walked into the pub which was deserted except for
Jethroe at the bar. 'What will you drink?' he asked.

'A glass of fresh lemonade, if that's possible?'

'Certainly is.'

Harry watched the publican make the drink and was
impressed when Jethroe added sugar syrup rather than
granulated sugar that never seemed to melt. Jethroe
pulled a pint of bitter for himself and placed it in front
of him on the bar. 'How are things going, sir?' he asked.

'Well, we're covering a great deal of territory and
everything we learn here is contributing in some way. I'd
like to ask you a few questions. Let's start with where
you were the night of the murder. No fancy stories,
Jethroe. Be brief and to the point.'

'I went on a bender with a couple of guys and then to
a local whore. Stayed the night.'

'I assume you have witnesses to that?' asked Harry,
who was already bored and irritated with questioning
Jethroe because he was certain the publican was lying.

'Yes,' he answered, a self-satisfied grin on his face.

'Who was the man in your cap and jacket walking

your dogs in the early hours of the morning when the postman discovered the abandoned car?'

'No one else walks my dogs. The postman must have got that wrong. They were with me in the back of my Range Rover that night. My hat and my jacket? No way could anyone else have been wearing them. I was.'

'And I suppose you can prove that?'

'Certainly I can.'

'Then who could it have been in the wood that morning?'

'A poacher. We have a terrible time with them round here. The gamekeeper from the Park can verify that.'

'Jethroe, you're a lying bastard.'

'Now, now! A detective like you in your hand-made suit and a fresh orchid in your lapel, I'd have expected better language and a little more respect for the public you serve. I'll put it down to frustration because you have no leads on Lady Olivia's whereabouts. Prove your accusation, sir,' snapped Jethroe.

'I don't have to do that. You're too mouthy, Jethroe. A thug trying to be a gentleman publican. Whatever you were doing that night, I doubt it had anything to do with Lady Olivia. I have learned a great deal about the lady and one thing is for sure: she would never have put her life in your hands. Not for a second. She was clever about people and would have seen, as I do, that your ego would one day have led you to brag about your role in the disappearance of Lady Olivia Cinders.

'You run a good pub, you're a terrific publican. Stick to that and not what you really did that night. Pike's a good detective. I think I'll leave him to question you about it further.'

Harry slammed a five-pound note on the counter and said, 'For the lemonade and your drink.' Then he walked away and out of the pub. There was a great deal to think about: his case, falling in love with September, these strange few days in Sefton Under Edge where nothing was as it seemed to be.

Walking through the village, he greeted several people and was calmed by the bird song, the warmth of the day, the sun that bathed the village in soft yellow light. Pieces of the mystery seemed to settle into a pattern he had not seen before. He watched the ducks for some time before he felt a yearning for tea at Miss Marble's.

The bell on top of the door tinkled as Harry entered the tea room. There were several middle-aged women sitting at a table over cups of tea. Locals who had lived there all their lives, they nodded a greeting to Harry then returned to their gossip. He knew from Joe and Jenny, who had interviewed them, who they were and how they felt about Olivia. He remembered that every one of these plain and simple people had at one time or another been indebted to Olivia for some act of kindness or generosity.

Joe Sixsmith had summed it up. 'For the locals, Olivia was their celebrity. She brought home to Sefton Under Edge the jet set people usually seen in *Hello* magazine at the hairdresser's. She was the beauty they aspired to be, living a riotous life at Sefton Park with the eccentric Buchanans. One of them even commented, "They're the Bloomsbury set of today: talented, eccentric, fun loving, and frighteningly intelligent." '

Miss Marble came into the room from the kitchen. She smiled at Harry. 'Tea?'

'Oh, yes, please.'

'And an assortment of cream cakes glazed with dark Belgian chocolate. How would that suit you, Chief Inspector?'

'To perfection, Miss Marble.'

Harry took a seat by the window and watched what little traffic there was pass by. His mind was a blank, just drifting in space and time while subconsciously he placed the pieces of his investigation together to solve the puzzle of what had happened to Lady Olivia.

A very elderly woman pushed her bicycle along the cobbled walk and leaned it against the window. She looked at Harry and smiled an apology for interrupting his view with the two-wheeler. She had one of the loveliest faces he had ever seen. Age had been kind to it. Every wrinkle seemed only to soften her beauty. She had deep violet eyes. Her white hair looked like spun sugar and she wore it in a shoulder-length bob. She was dressed in wide white linen trousers and a white blouse with long sleeves. She was an enchantress even now in her advanced years. Her body was slim, youthful, and her walk more of a stride. On her head she wore a somewhat battered straw hat with a wide brim. Her eyes were skilfully made up but she wore no other make-up save for a pale lipstick that was nearly transparent. Her soft skin was a pale creamy colour, and nearly translucent. She had a long slender neck and around it wore an ancient Roman coin set in a circle of gold and mounted on a black silk cord worn as a choker. Harry had recognised her at once as Miss Plumm, the oldest lady living in Sefton Under Edge. She was revered by everyone it seemed.

She entered the shop and the gossiping women rose from their chairs and went to greet her. Harry heard suggestions that she should join them. She graciously declined and was saved by the appearance of Miss Marble. The two women spoke and then the proprietor walked her over to Harry's table. He rose from his chair and having been introduced to Miss Plumm, kissed her hand and offered her a chair. She removed her hat and took a seat.

'I thought you might enjoy having tea together. The Chief Inspector has a sweet tooth, Miss Plumm,' announced Miss Marble.

'I hope I'm not intruding? I do apologise if so,' said Miss Plumm.

'You're not intruding. I'd be delighted to have your company.'

'But you would have had it this evening anyway. I'm invited to dinner at Marguerite Chen's. I must admit I have been very curious about the detectives from New Scotland Yard. You're not at all what I'd expected.' And Miss Plumm laughed. It was a seductive, charming sound. Like silver bells, thought Harry.

'And when had you proposed to interview me about the night of the murder?' she asked.

Harry noticed a glint in her eye. 'You're very to the point, Miss Plumm.'

'Not always, Chief Inspector,' she replied mysteriously.

Miss Marble arrived at the table with a fresh pot of tea and a slice of lemon tart with a dollop of clotted cream on the side for Miss Plumm. 'I don't think you'll be able to manage the pudding and your bicycle, Miss Plumm. I'm sure the Chief Inspector would be pleased to carry it for you, wouldn't you?'

Harry hardly heard what Miss Marble was saying, he was so distracted by Miss Plumm's hands. They were beautiful, not a liver spot on them, slender, with long fingers and oval fingernails. She used them eloquently, the way a ballerina entices with her arms as she creates wonders with her feet. There was something altogether mysterious and enchanting about Miss Plumm. Harry wanted to know her, what she had done with her eighty odd years. She was a romantic figure, more than just the oldest inhabitant of Sefton Under Edge.

Harry heard Miss Marble say, 'The pudding, Chief Inspector? Will you carry it for Miss Plumm?'

He snapped to attention and said, 'With great pleasure.'

'You needn't bring it now. Why don't you come with your colleagues for an apéritif and we can all go to Marguerite's together, pudding and all? It's to be my contribution to the dinner party.'

And so it was decided.

Chapter 11

Not being with Harry was no easy thing for September. She knew that they were not really estranged, would never break away from each other over her feelings about Olivia and Harry's having to bring her to justice. She also knew it had been unfair of her to ask him to let Olivia go, but hell, life wasn't fair.

She was in her studio, thinking about Harry and what their life was going to be like when they were living together. There was one thing for sure – when Harry returned to London she intended to go with him. That resolved in her mind, she placed her paint brush in the jug where they were kept, called the pub and asked to be put through to him. She had to be kept waiting on the line for a considerable time because the telephone was constantly engaged.

Jethroe told her, 'I think something has happened, a breakthrough of some kind, because the two detectives assisting the Chief have been burning up the telephone lines. Never off them for a minute.'

September was still holding the line when James and Harry entered the studio. She began to laugh, holding out the phone and shaking it vehemently. 'I've been waiting for ages to get through to you, and – hey presto, here you are.'

Quite suddenly her laughter vanished and she grew pale. 'Has something happened? Something terrible? Why are you together? Olivia . . . oh, God, you've not found her dead?' September backed away from the two men until she was against the wall.

Harry rushed to her. With his hands firmly gripping her upper arms, he shook her and said, 'No. Whatever made you think that? On the contrary, she's been sighted several times.' And he pulled September into his arms and kissed her, stroked her hair and kissed her again.

The colour came back into her face. 'I thought I had my fear for her under control,' she told them shakily.

James went to his sister and said as he gave her a brotherly kiss on the cheek, 'I was just showing Harry to the studio. Be kind to yourself and don't expect miracles, Sept. None of us will get over Olivia's disappearance for years, if ever. Accept that it's going to be that way and let's get on with our lives.'

There was no question in Harry's mind that James was right. For the first time he saw the suffering that Olivia's friends were going through, and because he was in love with September could hardly bear her pain which had become his. But what difference did that make in the pursuit of justice? None. Fortunately he was a man trained to separate the emotional side of his nature from his work. Harry was a man with real strength of character, an iron will.

'You seem suddenly far away, what are you thinking?' September asked.

'That James is right.' And Harry walked from her to her brother and the two men shook hands.

'I must run,' James said. 'I need to get away from all this and carry on with my life. I'm assembling an expedition in search of the rare butterflies of Guyana. There's a great deal of planning before we go on one of these treks. If I start setting it up now we could be off within the next six months.'

Harry and September watched him leave the studio. Once more, Harry felt as if he belonged in Sefton Park. That fate, not Olivia, had brought him to this place. He walked back to the woman he loved and took her in his arms. 'Come and live with me in London? I don't think that I could bear to leave you here.'

'I've been packed and ready to go, mentally at least, since the first time you touched me. Now it's only a matter of physically getting my things together. I'm not easy to live with, as I'm sure you've figured out. Painting's my life in the same way as justice is yours. I can't cook. I earn quite a bit of money but I'm extravagant. Can you live with that?'

'Sounds like bliss to me,' was his answer.

They kissed. Passion took over that kiss, and love, and a sense of oneness that was overwhelming.

Harry was enthralled by September's studio, one of the most gracious and at the same time exciting rooms he had ever been in. The room was two storeys high, what must once have been the ballroom of the house in its grander days, the many-paned oriel windows to either end of the room flooding it with light. But the paintings were what made the studio truly exciting. Large and rich with colour, abstract but with such refinement and passion, mystery and intrigue. They were potent with life; even the dark ones that should have been dull had an uplifting power about them, a sense of rebirth and a new ascendancy. They were intensely romantic.

Harry walked away from that passionate and extraordinary young woman to view them. September could see he was genuinely overwhelmed by her work and with an understanding of it that gladdened her heart. She followed him around the room and after a considerable time, when they were both swept away by the thrill of experiencing fine works of art, she skipped in front of him and began turning around paintings that had been facing the wall.

They had hardly had time together to discover each other, so swift had been their falling in love. Now Harry was learning more about her through her work than he ever could have discovered if they had been together for weeks, possibly months. She was more much more than he could have hoped for. She was that one in a million woman with talent and beauty, brains and a taste for the erotic.

'I am besotted with you and your work,' he told her finally.

'I love you, Harry. If not for Olivia we might never have met. You might never have found Sefton Under Edge. We might have missed the most important event of our lives.'

Olivia too had eaten into his life. She would always be

there. He had been smitten with her before he had met September and knew that Olivia was not done with him. He would always be smitten with her until the day he finally caught her and brought her to justice.

Now he wanted the taste of September in his mouth. He was thirsty for her orgasms, hungry to fuck her. He had no need even to tell her that; lust for her transformed his face like a mask. September took him by the hand and led him over to the chaise near the west window. There they undressed and lay down in each other's arms.

There was a dew drop of come on the tip of his rampant penis. September licked it away. 'We mustn't do this, not now, as much as I want you,' he told her.

'Why not?'

'Look.' A red sun was slowly setting, casting a pale pink light over the room and their entwined bodies. 'I don't want to fuck you and leave you. We need time so that I can make you come and come and come. And at the moment I don't have that time, I have things to work out before we go to Marguerite's for dinner.'

September placed a kiss on his lips. It was sweet and filled with passion. She trailed her kisses down his body to the base of his penis then licked it to the very tip. Slowly and deliberately she sucked him into her mouth and fondled his testes. He slid on to his back and September stood astride him and impaled herself upon his penis. With hands on her hips she rode up and down on Harry, all the time whimpering with pleasure. He felt the rush of her orgasms as she leaned forward and kissed him wildly. Harry was in a state of sexual ecstasy. His own orgasm was copious and release brought him perfect pleasure. He closed his eyes and drifted into oblivion for a few seconds. His heart was racing. He tore at her hair as he pulled September to him to suck on her nipples, fondle her breasts.

After a few minutes, just long enough to get a modicum of control over themselves, September pulled Harry off the chaise and started to dress him. His shirt first, then his tie. He stopped her. She smiled at him when he told her, 'I don't want to leave you.'

She slapped his hands lightly and went back to buttoning his shirt. 'I don't want you to leave me either. But we must start as we mean to go on. I'm sure this isn't going to be the only quickie we'll ever have, and I quite like adventurous sex. We have full lives to live, Harry. Work, fun, love . . . a lifetime in front of us.'

'Marry me?' he asked.

The offer of marriage quite overwhelmed September. Tears came into her eyes. She gave up dressing him and sat down to watch him complete the task. They never took their eyes off one another. 'Tell me you love Sefton Park and the village enough to make it our country house? I could never leave it, Harry.'

'You didn't answer my question, September. Just say yes.'

'You didn't answer mine,' was the only answer she gave him.

Together they both said, 'Yes,' and rushed into each other's arms. Afterwards they walked from the studio through the house, arm in arm, and agreed they would make no announcement of their engagement until they were set up in London. Their relationship was still intensely private and they wanted to keep it that way for as long as they could.

'About tonight at Marguerite Chen's. If I seem aloof, please realise that it's because I'm working and I have to switch off my emotions when on official business,' Harry warned.

September stood on tiptoe and pulled his head down to hers. She whispered, 'I've already seen you in work mode, you needn't have said anything about it. That split personality, the brilliant sleuth and the passionate lover, is the real you. I'm in love with both parts of you. Now give me a kiss and get on with whatever you have to do.' They kissed and September, heart filled with joy, ran away from him laughing.

When he unlocked his car, Harry saw the large cake box sitting on the front passenger seat. It reminded him of Miss Plumm whom he had yet to interview. He was more curious about her than suspicious. As he drove past her cottage he noted it was quite large and her garden utterly charming. There were lights on in the house and the yellow glow of dusk gave the place an intensely romantic look. She stuck in his mind as he continued on his way to the pub.

There were people drinking in The Fox, Jethroe and Hannah busy serving. Jethroe, having seen Harry enter the pub, watched him as he headed for the stairs and followed Harry. 'May I have a word?'

'Be quick about it, Jethroe. I have a great deal to do in a short period of time. And, by the way, we'll be pulling out of here late tomorrow afternoon.'

'About the talk we had earlier today . . .'

'That's over and done with. I thought you understood, I no longer consider you a suspect.'

'Maybe I could swop you some information if you could forget to call Chief Inspector Pike.'

'There's nothing you could tell me that would be of interest, Jethroe. Sorry, no deal.' And Harry walked away from him.

He heard a muffled, 'Prick!' and smiled as he took the stairs two at a time.

Joe seemed to be drowning in faxes, Jenny lost between stacks of paper, and both of them were still on the telephone. Harry scribbled a note that he was going to bath and change. He ordered a malt whisky and when Hannah arrived with it was only half dressed. He could not help but notice a fresh bruise on her cheek. She touched it, and her face reddened with embarrassment.

'You must have scared Jethroe half to death. He's told us all to be particularly nice to you.'

'Well, he'd better be particularly nice to *you*, and keep his business legal and above board.'

'Thanks,' she said.

'For what?'

'For giving me back my dignity. I gave in my notice last night. That's how I got this. He really can't help it. If I were to stay with him he would always do it to me because I let him get away with it that first time.'

'Where will you go?' asked a concerned Harry.

'I don't know.'

He walked to the table and took one of his calling cards, writing down his home number. He handed it to Hannah, telling her, 'If you're ever in trouble, or need anything, call me.'

The young girl, tears in her eyes, rushed to Harry and gave him a hug of gratitude. Then she stood back and, after wiping her eyes, asked, 'Is there anything more you want, sir?'

'No, Hannah. Thank you.'

Once dressed again, he sat down and sipped his drink. His mind was on Olivia and how she'd got away, so cleanly and so fast. The more details he learned, the more certain he was that not only was the murder of the prince premeditated but so was her escape. He rose from his chair, finished his drink in one swallow and went to see his assistants.

'No more calls, and switch those phones off. I want to know what you've found out about these South African sightings.'

Joe began, 'The tract of land is owned by Lady Olivia. The prince bought it for her when they visited South Africa two years ago, as a birthday gift. She wanted it for a game reserve, but never got around to doing anything with it. That information came from the Chief of Police of the surrounding area. That tract is called the Lalabella Reserve. The security guards report any problems that arise there to the Chief of Police and he reports them to Sir Thomas Redburn. Redburn is the wealthiest Englishman living in South Africa. He packs a great deal of power and deals with anything to do with the Lalabella Reserve. There's been nothing for him to do yet. As far as the Chief of Police, Walter Tombey, knows, Lady Olivia Cinders was only there once with the prince who took her on a tour of the area. They were joined on safari by the President of South Africa and the prince's younger brother. Tombey met her that once and has never heard of or seen her since.

'His office claims that the fax we received was not sent from them. We checked with Sir Thomas Redburn's office and reached him at his home. Both claim they did not send the fax about Lady Olivia being sighted in South Africa, but clearly someone sent it from somewhere nearby, either because she is there and they want us to catch her or it's a bogus fax sent in the hope that New Scotland Yard will grab the bait and fly down there on a fruitless hunt,' said Jenny.

'What would be the advantage to Lady Olivia if we had taken the bait? If it *is* bait,' asked Joe.

'She would be buying time to settle in where she really is, probably on the other side of the world: the jungles of Mexico or some South American country. She could be anywhere, if she's still alive. She's a very clever lady who has been planning this for some time and so far is foxing us brilliantly,' said Harry.

No one said a word. He was surprised at the despondent expressions on their faces. He did not feel at all defeated. 'Why such glum faces?' he asked.

'Frankly, sir, I thought we might have done better here. We haven't come up with one substantiated clue. I can't see that we've got anywhere.'

'Haven't got anywhere? I think you and Jenny had

better study your notes and do some serious detecting. Examine closely what you have learned about the elusive Lady Olivia while you dress for dinner.'

'What am I supposed to wear, sir? This isn't my sort of thing. I'll feel out of place, downright insecure with those upper-class beauties. It's very out of line for us to accept such an invitation.'

'Sullivan, go and get dressed! I detest that "poor little me" attitude so get rid of it – *now*!' said Harry, irritated with his assistant. It never ceased to amaze him that that old chestnut of the class system was still a problem for some people.

As the two detectives were leaving the sitting-room, Harry announced, 'Marguerite Chen thinks she is giving a dinner and is in control of events this evening but we three know we have only agreed to be there because we'll be working. I expect to learn what really happened on the night of the murder and to decide where we go from here.'

While his associates were dressing for what now looked as if it would be a fascinating turn of events, Harry made several calls to South Africa, the last of which was to Sir Thomas Redburn. Amazingly Sir Thomas recognised the Graves-Jones name. He had been to university with Harry's Uncle Raymond.

They talked about Uncle Raymond of whom Sir Thomas had been a lifelong friend, even though they only rarely saw each other. The conversation finally turned to the reason for Harry's call: Lady Olivia Cinders. Sir Thomas did, of course, know about the fax after Joe's call but could not shed any light on the matter. It remained yet another mysterious development in the murder investigation.

'If you don't mind my asking, Sir Thomas, how did you come to be in control of the Lalabella Reserve in Lady Olivia's absence?' asked Harry.

'That was what the prince and she wanted. It's not the sort of place that can be left to drift along without hands-on authority to control it. I arranged security for them, turned it into a private country all of its own. You see, I have always loved Lalabella, and sold it to the prince on condition he would keep it as it is, wild and wonderful. He and Lady Olivia were staying with me and when I took them to see Lalabella, she fell in love with the place, and whatever Olivia wanted the prince gave her. She was one of the most enchanting women I have ever met. Such a pity she didn't just leave the prince but had to kill him.'

'Then you believe she's guilty!' asked a surprised Harry.

'Oh, yes. You see, they had a very volatile relationship – love and hate. They lived a depraved sexual life from which she could not escape. A tragedy, the whole sordid affair.'

'Do you believe she's hiding out in Lalabella?'

'Without my knowing it? Well, I doubt that. But if she has found her way there, you'd never find her. She'd be like a queen in her own kingdom, knowing every move you made. It would come down to who was stalking who. No, she's too clever to chance Lalabella as a hideaway. You have to remember, you're not the only one on the hunt for her. The prince's brother has vowed to track her down, put her on trial in his country and publicly hang her. Lalabella is the first place he'd search for her. I told him it was a waste of time, that if I found her there I would turn her over to him. He believed me. I have been a good friend to his family, they trust me and my word.'

'I wouldn't like you to do that, Sir Thomas,' warned Harry.

'Have no fear, I'll keep an eye out for her. But, my dear boy, you have my word I will never find her,' said Sir Thomas. Two Englishmen making a gentleman's agreement.

'Thank you for being so candid with me, Sir Thomas.'

'Come and visit some time, my boy. Big house, eighteen bedrooms, and Cape Town is very beautiful. Your Uncle Raymond enjoyed stopping off here from his travels. That lady he always travelled with – can't remember her name – she had the same beauty and charm, was enchanting in exactly the same way as Olivia. I never understood why Raymond let her get away. Oh, well, old memories. They make one feel young again, at least for a few minutes. Goodbye, old boy.'

Harry rang off and sat for several minutes thinking about Raymond. It had never occurred to him that his uncle had travelled with a woman. Harry had always thought him to be a confirmed bachelor, a man who'd had his fair share of women when he'd wanted them, but never had he imagined that there was one special lady whom Raymond took on his travels. Uncle and nephew were far closer than father and son and yet Raymond had never mentioned that he had a female travelling companion. Harry was wondering why his uncle had kept her such a deep, dark secret? Had he finally abandoned her, or had she abandoned him? He was thinking how much he would have liked to have known her when Jenny and Joe arrived in the sitting-room.

Chapter 12

Once Miss Plumm had left Harry behind in Miss Marble's tea room, she gave a sigh of relief, mounted her bicycle and slowly pedalled home. For days she had been prepared for the moment when she would come face to face with him, having recognised the Graves-Jones name. Intuition told her he was Raymond's much-loved nephew. She could not imagine that he could be anyone else for how many men in England could there be called Harry Graves-Jones?

Her first sight of him through the tea room window had made her heart skip a beat, he looked so much like Raymond. Then, while having tea with him, she'd recognised many of Raymond's gestures. It seemed to her as if her long-time lover had been reincarnated, certainly in spirit if not in body.

Once home she lay down on her bed to take her usual late-afternoon nap. But sleep would not come. Memories of her life with Raymond Graves-Jones came flooding back to keep her awake. They had been together for fifteen wonderful years. Both keen travellers, that was how they met: at the Winter Palace in Luxor, Upper Egypt.

Miss Plumm had led an exciting life both before and after she'd met and left Harry's Uncle Raymond, but it was rare for her to look back on it. She was not a woman to dwell on her past and grow old with nothing but memories to keep her young. Nor was she one who lived and dined out on past experiences. She rose from her bed with a smile on her face, laughter on her lips, and went to her dressing-table. She took a long look in the mirror, liked what she saw and began to do up her hair for the evening.

Having finished her hair and make-up, Miss Plumm went to her wardrobe and selected what she would wear. She settled for a long, deep blue silk taffeta skirt, a burnt orange silk top, and a wide turquoise sash. She wore no jewellery: not a ring on her finger, not a bauble on her ear, not a single bracelet, merely a choker of large pearls. She was dressing for what she expected to be a most interesting evening. When Marguerite had invited her she'd said, 'Anthea, I'm giving a dinner and want you to come. The New Scotland Yard people will be here, as well as September, James and Angelica, and a few others.'

Anthea Plumm almost never went out in the evening. When she did it was to dine with the Buchanans at Sefton Park or to Marguerite's house. On the rare occasions when she had people in, they were always the same crowd. She checked herself once more in the mirror and was not displeased.

She knew the women would dress for dinner and look sublime, they always did, and that James would have dressed in black tie and dinner jacket. The Buchanans always dressed for dinner. Miss Plumm slipped her feet into black satin slippers and very carefully walked down the stairs, turned on the lights and set out four champagne flutes for Harry, herself, and his colleagues. She opened a decorative tin and from it removed cheese straws she had made the day before and carefully arranged them on a silver salver.

Just then she heard a knock at the front door which she had left ajar and Harry's voice: 'Miss Plumm, it's Harry Graves-Jones and colleagues.'

'Do come in,' she said as she walked from the kitchen through to the drawing-room, carrying the silver salver.

Introductions were made and she asked him if he would mind carrying the silver wine cooler in from the kitchen for her. 'Too heavy for me, I'm afraid.'

Joe wanted to say something but was too much in awe of Miss Plumm and her drawing-room to open his mouth. It was left to Jenny to make conversation. 'What an interesting room, Miss Plumm, and so many fascinating photographs. Would you mind if I took a tour to look at them?'

Harry heard the tail end of Jenny's request. He had taken in the room the moment he entered the house. It had a singular atmosphere that was enchanting but difficult to figure out. It was old-fashioned, the typical English country cottage one might have seen before the Second World War: all faded flowered chintz and handsome stripes on the upholstered pieces. But it wasn't quite that because it also had marvellous furniture and paintings, and a concert grand piano in a bow window overlooking the garden. The furniture consisted of fine English antiques and amazingly beautiful oriental carpets, Chinese bowls of fresh flowers beautifully arranged on nearly every table and photographs in silver frames everywhere.

Harry placed the silver cooler on the table indicated by Miss Plumm who asked him to open the bottle of vintage Roederer Cristal, the Rolls-Royce of champagnes. Joe Sixsmith found his voice and started talking to Miss Plumm which gave Harry a chance to think about her. He passed the filled glasses and found it odd that every photograph he saw was topographic: wonderful ancient archaeological sites from all round the world with Miss Plumm the only person featured in them.

Small photographs, big, medium-sized, and in not one of them another human being. Harry raised his glass and made a toast. 'To Miss Plumm and absent friends.'

She smiled and sipped from her glass. Harry sensed that the elderly lady was the most intensely private person he had ever met. She was a world unto herself. He was fascinated by her because she was like a diamond: multi-faceted. Harry thought that she was not just one thing but another and another. For example, he knew her to have been born in Sefton Under Edge and that her father had been Sefton Park's head gardener during James's grandfather's time. How did she go from being a simple country girl to a well-spoken, elegant grande dame who'd travelled the world?

'You were obviously a keen traveller, Miss Plumm.'

'I still am,' she replied.

'Even now? How courageous of you,' said an admiring but not very subtle Jenny.

Harry shot her a fierce look and Miss Plumm laughed. 'You mean, because of my advanced years? You mustn't feel you have made a blunder, my dear, I'm not offended. I have always been an adventurer and enjoyed the far-flung places of this world. It just takes me a great deal longer to get around them now.'

'How often do you travel, Miss Plumm?' asked Joe.

'Once or twice a year, depending how I'm feeling. I only travel when I sense that the body and the mind are ready to go.'

'Are you planning any journeys now, Miss Plumm?' asked Harry.

'Yes, I am.'

He was aware that she had no intention of saying where she was going and to ask her seemed like an intrusion, something he was loath to do. He had a strange sensation that he had been in this room before. Of course he hadn't. But there were so many easily recognisable objects: Greek bronzes, a stone sculpture of an Egyptian god, an ivory reclining Japanese lady, a Russian samovar, a Tibetan prayer wheel. The whole room somehow had a familiar stamp to it that was reminiscent of his own sitting-room in Albany.

Instinct suddenly took him over and the question had to be asked. 'Miss Plumm, am I not right in guessing you are a very close friend of Lady Olivia Cinders?'

'You are most certainly correct, I am.'

Miss Plumm rose from her chair and, taking the bottle of champagne from the cooler, went to him to refill his glass. 'May I call you Harry?' she asked.

'Yes, please do,' was his reply.

'Harry, will you top up everyone's glass, please?'

Jenny Sullivan could barely take her eyes off Miss Plumm. They had been here in this room with the elderly lady for no more than twenty minutes and already she had the three of them eating out of her hand. How had she managed to do that? There was no doubt she had a seductive charm. Miss Plumm was beautiful, enchanting. How was it possible for a woman her age to have so much sensual appeal? Jenny could only wonder how many hearts she had broken in her youth, how many men must have loved her. What a life she must have led. There was no doubting that.

Joe was impressed with the way Miss Plumm answered his superior's question while at the same time dismissing him, thus making it impossible for him to ask any more about Lady Olivia's relationship with her and whether she had seen Lady Olivia on the night of the murder.

Miss Plumm most charmingly turned the tables on the detectives when she asked them, 'How have you found us? Are we a microcosm of the world? I often think we're just more clever at hiding ourselves than most. And our dear Olivia who has always, since childhood, played a starring role among very nearly every one of the families here ... has she crept into your hearts? I'm sure she has, even though you are her enemy, she your quarry.'

Miss Plumm kicked back the hem of her skirt. The swish of the silk taffeta was a charmingly feminine statement that accentuated the regal stance she had taken. She walked away from the bemused detectives.

Standing at the fireplace, she addressed Jenny first. 'You, Detective Constable Sullivan – I would imagine the more you learn about Olivia, the more uncomfortable you feel? That's not her fault but yours. You must not be resentful of her. She is for you a murderer, after all, not a woman to envy.

'Detective Constable Sixsmith, I sense you feel you are being held back, are frustrated because you have not been allowed to use a more direct and adversarial approach in investigating this case. We've only just met and so you will wonder how I have deduced that. Quite easily, actually. You are young and ambitious to climb the career ladder and so had been determined to look upon Olivia not as a human being but as a case you have to solve. You hate her for eluding you and are angry with her friends who love her and are unable to give her up to you. But my dear Detective Constable Sixsmith – we can't give you what we don't have.

'Now, on the other side of the coin, so to speak, we have Detective Chief Inspector Graves-Jones who by now knows a great deal about Olivia. He is naturally besotted with her because to know her is to love her, flaws and all. New Scotland Yard has been very clever in choosing him to head the investigation because if anyone can work out the disappearance of Olivia and find her, it will be him.'

Jenny and Joe were lost for words. The three detectives

knew that Miss Plumm was spot on in everything she had said. They could not understand why she had set them on edge with her analysis of the situation. Why had she turned the tables on them? Harry was sure she had intended to do that when she'd invited them for a drink. Well, she had succeeded. She had turned from a fascinating little woman of considerable age to a bold and frank one who obviously felt the detectives needed a dressing down.

It was Harry who broke the silence while their hostess drained her glass. 'Miss Plumm, have you ever been to South Africa?' he asked, clearly putting an end to what she'd had to say and killing any possibility of further discussion.

Miss Plumm, ignoring Harry's question, placed her glass on the silver tray and, turning to her guests, suggested, 'As nice as it is to have you all here, I fear we must leave for Marguerite's house and dinner.'

It was decided that Joe and Jenny should go in one car and Miss Plumm and the cake box in Harry's. He moved it from the front to the rear and helped Miss Plumm into the passenger seat. As they drove in convoy up to Marguerite's house, Harry was aware of the beauty of the night. It was warm and balmy, with a moon that was nearly full and casting a glistening white light on the park. The black sky was studded with a myriad stars. The faint scent of jasmine filled the car. 'It's a marvellously romantic night and your scent . . . it makes me think of Alexandria,' he told her.

'Yes, one of my favourite cities,' she answered.

'Miss Plumm, you never answered my question. Have

you ever been to South Africa?'

'Yes, I have, many times.'

'Cape Town?' he pressed.

'Yes, Cape Town. Now I think we should leave it at that. I much prefer interesting conversation to questions.'

Miss Plumm was a woman who guarded her privacy, liked to keep her secrets to herself, that was clear. But Harry had never met anyone who knew how to do it with such determination and subtle style. There was something about her that intrigued him: that split personality, the country villager and the sophisticated, well-bred traveller.

'One more question?' he pleaded.

'If you must,' she replied, a lovely smile on her lips. She was playing with Harry and thoroughly enjoying herself.

'In your travels, did you ever come across my Uncle, Raymond Graves-Jones?' he ventured.

'One meets so many people while travelling. Ah, and here we are,' she said, grazing his cheek with the back of her hand. There was unmistakable affection in that gesture and he was surprised to find how much it meant to him.

He helped Miss Plumm from the car and then retrieved the cake box from the rear seat. She watched his every move, actually very charmed by the quality of the man, his handsomeness. She liked the cut and thrust of him, his subtle approach, his intelligence, that he was sensitive enough to appreciate who and what Olivia was. If any man could find her and bring her to justice it would most certainly be Harry Graves-Jones, backed up by the power of New Scotland Yard. But she knew in her heart, as the others gathering in the house knew, that that would never happen. Olivia, if she were still alive, would never allow herself to be captured.

Fate was playing games with Harry and being very good to Anthea Plumm for she had never expected to meet her lover's nephew. It was, in an odd sort of way, like meeting Raymond again. In the years she had travelled with him she had learned about Harry through his uncle's love and devotion to his nephew. But Harry had never become a part of her life. Raymond and Anthea had had a very strange relationship. They never once, in all their years of love and friendship, lived together in England. Neither one of them had any interest in that. Raymond liked being a famous and well-respected judge and enjoyed the social set he moved in occasionally ... And Anthea? She insisted on no more than their being together when they were travelling. Yet they loved each other, were romantic lovers who could only escape through travel. They were not a couple who could have survived a more mundane life.

Escorting Miss Plumm into the house and balancing the cake at the same time was made no easier by Harry's being distracted with thoughts of Olivia. There was something so strange about the way this evening was developing. He was working out why and the moment they entered the house, began to laugh. Miss Plumm looked at him and smiled. Jenny looked confused and

Joe was busy trying to work out what his superior had to laugh about.

'Sir?' he said.

'We've been terribly dense about this evening, Sixsmith. This isn't a dinner and dance affair, more dinner and a show-down. As in a Western movie. *Gunfight at the OK Corral.*'

Joe seemed more confused than ever but not Miss Plumm or Marguerite who had come forward to greet them. 'I'm rather glad you've worked it out, Chief Inspector,' their hostess told Harry and then kissed Miss Plumm.

She suggested that they put the cake box in the kitchen and so that was where Harry followed her. He undid the satin bow on the large box. 'Better let me lift the cake out while you hold the box. It's so sweet of Anthea to bring the pudding for this meal. It was she who taught Miss Marble how to make it,' Marguerite told him.

After greeting everyone, Miss Plumm arrived in the kitchen and stood next to Harry. She watched the pudding emerge from its box. Harry was astonished. It was a Pavlova: a honey-coloured meringue base with plump meringue roosting birds all round it and filled with fresh glazed raspberries. An astonished Harry looked from the Pavlova to Miss Plumm. She nodded, smiled, and gave a charming peal of laughter, then walked round the wooden table and patted him on the shoulder as she left the kitchen.

'Have I missed something? You'll have to tell me because Anthea never will. She does like her secrets and loves to tease, especially those who intrude on her privacy,' said Marguerite.

'I've already experienced that!' said Harry.

'Isn't the pudding magnificent? Miss Marble is such a great pastry chef, but especially when doing something for Anthea.'

Marguerite went to the refrigerator, removed a bowl of whipped cream and proceeded to cover the raspberries with it. Harry stood mesmerised by the pudding. It had been his uncle's favourite. That look Miss Plumm had given him when they'd gazed across it? It implied an answer to Harry's question about whether she had known his uncle. He understood now that she was the woman Sir Thomas Redburn had mentioned as being his Uncle Raymond's travelling companion. How clever she had been to let him discover that on his own. She must have known he would recognise the pudding. It was an exact replica of the one that had arrived every year on his birthday by messenger.

Harry was charmed to think of his uncle and Miss Plumm loving each other during secret liaisons two or three times a year. He felt something akin to deep affection and respect for Miss Plumm, wanting to keep her love affair with his uncle secret, a very precious thing. It would most certainly have been what his Uncle Raymond would have wanted or he would have told Harry about his 'travelling companion'. Harry could understand why they had kept their affair secret and sporadic; that way it was more romantic, exciting, new and fresh with every journey. It was both fantasy and real love, powerful and delicate.

James arrived in the kitchen with a malt whisky on the rocks and handed it to Harry. 'Anthea asked me to give you this, she thought you might appreciate it.'

'Miss Plumm is quite a lady,' said Harry as he took a long swallow of the golden liquid.

He walked into the drawing-room where James introduced him to everyone he did not already know. While talking with Angelica and September, it was as if he'd been hit by a bolt of lightning. Lady Olivia's accomplice, if she did indeed have one, had to have been Miss Plumm! It was pure instinct, but he was sure he was right. The faxes from South Africa? She could have arranged them, had been to Lalabella, loved and respected Olivia, and like the others wanted her never to be brought to justice.

'You seem suddenly to have drifted away from us, Harry?' Angelica observed.

'A sudden moment of intuition.'

'Can you share it with us?' asked September.

'Not for the moment. Maybe later this evening?'

Harry liked Angelica who had a more fragile beauty than September. She would most certainly not have ridden up to him on a white horse and seduced him. He saw her eyes dart to Neville Brett on several occasions in the short time he spent with the sisters. When James joined them it was to whisk Angelica away to meet someone. That gave Harry a few minutes alone with September.

'It's very difficult to keep quiet about us. I want to shout to the entire world how happy I am to love you. But prudence has suddenly come into my life along with love. I wouldn't like to compromise your position here. But the moment we have driven away from Sefton Under Edge, I'll shout it to the world,' September told him, only just restraining herself from slipping her arms around him and kissing him passionately.

Harry began to laugh. She was audacious, a free spirit, totally enticing to a man such as him. 'Not very much daunts me, September, but you people here in Sefton Park do. You're élitist, privileged, with the strangest set of morals I have ever come across. To marry you would be to become one of your unusual extended family: Miss Plumm, Marguerite, James, Angelica. Though I fear Neville and I will always be just outside the inner circle, never quite belong. But the rewards are great: love, passion, and you next to me for all my life.'

Harry could see tears of emotion in her eyes. Fighting them back, September told him, 'Oh, Harry, you forgot Olivia? She was the heart and soul of all of us for most of our lives. Ever since the death of the prince and her disappearance, everyone in this room has had their life turned upside down. I have met and fallen deeply in love with you, Angelica had been in a love triangle with Neville and Marguerite and has given him up and sent him with her blessings to Marguerite. Marguerite's in love with Neville and wants marriage, something she has run away from until now. And James has finally begun returning the calls of an American botanist, a Philadelphia socialite called Emily Warfield, who has been chasing him for years. And although I don't know them, I'm sure your detectives won't leave this place untouched, whereas you arrived here, my dear love, already changed by your manhunt for Olivia.'

At that moment Marguerite approached her guests to tell them, 'Dinner is served.'

Chapter 13

Anthea Plumm was seated at the dining table between James and Neville Brett. She gazed around it at each of Marguerite's guests. They were a handsome, intelligent group of people, even the three detectives. They shone, all of them, with youth and beauty, and had years ahead of them to live their lives to the full. All the things she no longer had or was able to do.

Where had it gone, her life? It seemed it was no more and probably less than a fraction of a second in the big picture of time and eternity. James and Neville engaged her in conversation alternately. She heard herself talking with them but it was like being on automatic pilot: she was there but not there. She was aware of everything: the ramshackle house for which Marguerite was notorious, books piled high on every surface, dead flowers in vases with an inch of stale water, manuscripts stacked everywhere, a desk piled high with fan mail, a marmalade cat the size of a small dog who strolled round the house and a St Bernard dog who behaved like a pussy cat.

The dining table was a *mélange* of mismatched porcelain that Marguerite had collected, matching crystal glasses, crisp white linen cloth and napkins. The food was delicious because Marguerite grew everything she could in her garden and was a marvellous cook. All this was being played out before Anthea's eyes and yet she seemed to be drifting away from it. Her past life kept infiltrating the scene around her. She was in a way quite frightened by what was happening because she was not usually one to look back and confuse her past with her present. It unnerved her, and she made a conscious effort to stop it. She couldn't. Quite suddenly she had lost control of her will to forget and move on.

James touched her arm, 'Are you all right, Anthea?' he asked.

Assuring him that she was, she redoubled her efforts to live in the moment and enjoy the evening. In vain. She tried to work out in her mind why this was happening to her. Olivia? It was true she was genuinely shocked by the murder of the prince and that Olivia was involved in that. There was not a day went by that she didn't think of Olivia on the run for the remainder of her life, and how she would have to live with the knowledge that she had taken a man's life. Anthea had loved her, had seen so much of herself in Olivia.

How different her own life had been! Everything had always come so easily to Olivia; so hard and so unfairly to Anthea. She was talking with her dinner partner Neville but at the same time running her life through her mind. It was like a picture show. She could hardly relate to some of the scenes flashing before her eyes. They had been her secrets and she was going to die with them.

She had been the Buchanans' head gardener's daughter, or so everyone had thought. In truth she was the gardener's wife's daughter. She was born, as they say, on the wrong side of the blanket. Her father had been the present Lord Buchanan's grandfather. Only her mother and His Lordship knew the truth of her birth, and then before she died Anthea's mother had told her she was the product of a passionate love affair that had lasted years. An upstairs-downstairs romance that her gardener-father must never know about. Anthea had Buchanan blood running through her veins.

As a child she had loved Sefton Park. She ran and played with the Buchanan children as well as the villagers', worked in the garden with her father and was taught by the various tutors hired for the Buchanan children. She wore Buchanan hand-me-downs, and learned her manners from Lady Buchanan as well as how to arrange flowers. Lost for a lifetime, all those idyllic days. Why, she wondered, were they coming back to haunt her now? Had those memories been triggered by the appearance of Raymond's beloved nephew? Was she remembering things past before advancing years were about to rob her of that luxury?

The first course arrived at the table via two village girls who worshipped Marguerite for her fame. They were her waitresses when she needed them, her under-gardeners, her post runners for those late manuscripts, articles, and charming rejections to lecture invitations she did not care to take on. They brought in two enormous broccoli soufflés, impressively high enough for Marguerite to receive an ovation. The girls went around the table serving; Neville rose from his chair and followed them, filling glasses with perfectly chilled Chablis. There was never a dull moment at Marguerite's table and the guests, fortified with drinks and wine, were animated and clearly enjoying themselves.

Anthea Plumm forked some soufflé into her mouth and sheer delight washed away her memories. She felt herself relaxing. She even told an amusing story about Marguerite's passion for gardening and most especially her *potager*. Everyone laughed and someone else took over with an amusing tale.

Once more Miss Plumm was distracted by the past. This time she was remembering the first time she saw Olivia's grandfather. She was a child of fifteen and unusually beautiful, innocent and vulnerable. It had been, for the young girl, love at first sight. He had been handsome and charming, a dashing figure of a man, an adventurer who made intrepid journeys to romantic places. The Cinderses and the Buchanans were great friends and the Cinderses, when His Lordship wasn't travelling, visited often. He had always had a soft spot for Plumm's little girl, watched her grow up and finally became besotted with her. She was a sensuous little thing: that charm of country girl combined with aristocratic mannerisms and speech enchanted him.

Anthea never hesitated for a minute when he asked her to run off with him. He had planned it carefully so that the scandal could be hushed up. No one in Sefton Park or Sefton Under Edge heard a word about it. So far as anyone knew the gardener's daughter had been sent to finishing school in Switzerland, a gift from the

Buchanans to a faithful servant's only child. In truth, they travelled the world for a year. He taught her how to dress, or rather the great Parisian couturiers taught her. A sensualist and libertine, Lord Wallingford Cinders taught her all things erotic, some of them depraved, and how to enjoy sex with total abandon. She never did understand that to him she was a plaything, a toy he would toss away when he tired of it.

He abandoned her in Venice, leaving her in the care of a Venetian count, one of his best friends, who saw her through the trauma of rejection on a grand scale, deception on an even greater one. That Wallingford had loved her she had no doubt, but he'd loved his long-suffering wife, his children and his freedom more. Olivia's grandfather was a cad with women but a well-mannered and generous one. He provided Anthea with a bank draft in her name for a tidy sum of money which would keep her for years. The count invested this wisely for her. Broken-hearted, it took her several months to come to terms with her situation, which she could never have done without the count's kindness and generosity.

She had not thought of that tumultuous time for more than sixty years. Now she smiled to herself. The experience had made her very strong and not unlike the man she'd loved. Anthea had always looked upon her life as being one driven by fate. She felt lucky to have loved with such passion and that, after decades, she should have experienced that again with Raymond Graves-Jones.

As suddenly as her memories had come flooding back,

they faded. Anthea sighed with relief. She was here and this was now and that sensation was like coming home from a long journey. She looked around the table and was astonished to think that she was intimately connected to so many of the guests round that table: the Buchanans, Olivia, who was certainly there in spirit, and Harry Graves-Jones. It was of course Olivia and her dreadful act that had brought them all together.

The girls had just finished serving the main course: poached salmon on a bed of steamed cucumber, Hollandaise sauce and coconut rice. Anthea rose from her chair and raised her glass. The others rose to join her. She announced, 'A toast to absent friends – may they be safe and well, wherever they are.'

Her friends were taken aback. It was unlike her to do anything so provocative. It was so obvious that she had meant the toast for Olivia. The three detectives were being made to understand that, no matter what, Olivia's friends would remain loyal to her in their hearts and minds.

Joe and Jenny were furious at the arrogance of Miss Plumm and Olivia's friends. If it were up to Joe he would put them all in their place, declare them an immoral lot and use the full power of the law to push them around a bit until someone gave them a clue to Olivia's whereabouts. And Jenny? She detested the lot of them, believing they were thumbing their noses at the law. It upset her that they had somehow outflanked the police and had better control of the situation than they did. Both the young detectives, quite prepared to walk out at that moment, looked to Harry for guidance.

'Hear, hear,' he said, and drank from his glass. The others round the table followed suit. Joe and Jenny reluctantly remained and raised their glasses.

General conversation resumed but there was a sudden change in the tone of the evening. Harry had ridden out the arrogance and gained control by being the first to join in the toast, wrongfooting Olivia's friends at the same time. Joe sensed the change and not for the first time was in awe of the way his superior's cunning and subtle approach worked.

The Pavlova was served and declared a wonder of a pudding. When not a morsel was left the guests adjourned to the drawing-room where the village girls served coffee and cognac. There was something quite beautiful and rare about the people draped around the room. Without even trying, they created an air of vivacity. Here were sensuous women and handsome men with an intelligence about them that was inspiring. It was not just in their looks, it was in their sureness of self, a grasp on life that made them able to spin any way they liked. Yes, they were privileged people but they worked at being privileged; it was not just a case of being born into it, it was using privilege to enrich their lives.

As Miss Plumm looked round the room she was proud of what her friends were doing with their lives, what they had learned from Olivia as she had learned from Olivia's grandfather and Harry's uncle: how to be a free spirit, to use everything to add and not take away from one's life. They were individuals who did not have to run with the crowd, follow the rules when those rules were wrong for them.

She looked at Harry and saw so much of his uncle in him. He was a special kind of man in the same way as Raymond had been. He had lived two lives simultaneously: that of a Superior Court Judge and the life of a man who liked to indulge himself in a world of erotic happenings once he had met Anthea. She had learned the joys of sexual freedom and bliss, sexual debauchery, even depravity, from Olivia's grandfather.

Once more the past danced into her brain and she was reminded of being young again, brave and courageous, when she and Raymond had been befriended by an Ottoman prince living in Alexandria in a palace on the sea. The man lived for nothing but sex and the excitement that went with the most adventurous, sometimes bizarre, kinds. For him such depravity was nothing more than a way of reaching oblivion. Under his influence, the staid, very conventional Englishman Judge Raymond Graves-Jones vanished when he and Anthea were behind closed doors.

For a few minutes, she relived a night on the Nile, sailing under a white crescent moon, having sex with Raymond and the prince. On a bed of cushions spread on the desk of the prince's yacht, she gave herself over completely to their sexual fantasies. They were no longer young but their sexual desires were. Erotic madness took them over and it had been a case of more, there must be more. Depravity took them over: bondage and tantalising light whippings that drove the three into another kind of sexual ecstasy. A handful of large oriental pearls inserted into her cunt gave Anthea enormous pleasure when she was riven by her lovers, such exquisite ecstasy that she was breathless from the many orgasms she had, one after the other. Her lovers insisted she wear her pearls in that manner for several days so as to enjoy having orgasms whenever she wanted them. It took nothing more than the squeezing of her most intimate muscles against the pearls.

Anthea began to laugh aloud and the memory faded with her laughter. She touched the pearl necklace round her throat, unable to stop laughing. It was September who pleaded, 'Oh, do share your joke with us,' as she went to Anthea and sat on the arm of her chair.

'Too private and personal, dear, but I will tell you one thing. We are all indebted to ourselves for the privileged life we have lived, for being courageous, by making our lives rich and full and packed with adventure, for following our dreams and desires, living in the moment and taking the consequences, good or bad.

'We all love and are indebted to Olivia because she was the bravest of us all in living life to the full and giving herself over to the ones she loved. It would be good for us to admit that we are much the same kind and might ourselves make a similar error in allowing ourselves to take a life. We must love ourselves for who and what we are. Poor Olivia. If she had loved herself more, she might never have turned to such a violent act.'

Marguerite rose from her seat and walked around the room to stand between Angelica and Neville. She felt extraordinarily happy. Her life was about to take another turn; she finally had the man in it she had always wanted but had never found till now.

Neville was besotted with Marguerite and although he

had meant not to be obvious about it, the way he looked at her revealed as much to everyone.

Angelica would always love Neville but she was relieved to have had the courage to give him up to the woman he loved. She had been aware of the couple's unhappiness at being apart for so long. It was no sacrifice for her, she was ready to move on in her career and needed love affairs that were frivolous and without commitment at this time in her life.

She whispered to Marguerite, 'What's happening to us? Our lives are turning upside down and new events are crashing in on us. I don't mind your announcing that you and Neville are now an item, bent on a future together.'

'You've always been the most generous of us, Angelica.' After kissing her affectionately on the cheek, Marguerite turned to her guests and said, 'Harry, ever since Olivia vanished from our lives and you and your team arrived in Sefton Under Edge, things around us have been spinning round out of control. The tragic turn of events in Olivia's life, and you and your team prying into ours, questioning our lifestyle, have made us understand that something fundamental is changing for us. I invited you and your colleagues here to dinner because, instead of all floundering around, I thought we should put our mutual concern for Olivia out in the open. Let's all play the truth game rather than a guessing game that keeps going off at tangents. That's no help to you or to us, and certainly does an injustice to Olivia. So let's examine every detail of your murder case and finally put it to rest.'

Harry's first reaction to Marguerite's taking control

of an ongoing case was of anger. The arrogance of Marguerite Chen! The sheer audacity of the woman and her suggestion. His second reaction was to realise what a formidable woman Marguerite was with her determination, her intelligence, those fine-boned and sensuous good looks. The dramatic aura she presented with that mass of silken black hair, provocative disposition and fiery nature, demanded she be a part of the intriguing mystery surrounding Lady Olivia Cinders.

Jenny Sullivan was not so forbearing. Angrily she got to her feet and declared: 'Is everything a game to you, Miss Chen? The sick and brutal murder of a man, an escaped murderess – just a game! Do you turn everything into something to play with so you don't have to face the unpalatable reality of it? You of all people, so admired, so intelligent when standing on your soapbox. Stop playing with this tragedy as if it is a game. It was a cruel, sick, depraved murder. Don't you read the newspapers?'

Harry went to Jenny and touched her arm. 'Come over here and sit with me. You too, Joe. I think it appropriate that we do as our hostess suggests and play her truth game.'

'Detective Constable Sullivan, I'm sorry if I've offended you. But I do believe that life unto death is a game one must play and win. Of *course* I play with life and do what I must to win. You're young and take things and situations too seriously. One can make life a game and achieve wonders. Has no one ever told you that? Shame on you, Harry.'

The little contretemps between Jenny and Marguerite

had made an impression on Joe. He felt as if someone had slapped his face. Everything had changed and he was aware as he had never been before. He saw exactly what Marguerite Chen meant. How incredibly easy life, work, love, were when you played them like a game, and always to win. He was astounded that he had never realised before that that was what he most admired in his superior, Harry Graves-Jones. The vintage car, the Savile Row suits, the truly unorthodox way in which he worked . . . all of it a game that Harry always won. He never resorted to self-indulgent seriousness to feed his ego. He did not feed his own vanity by seeing his role as that of Nemesis. He was careful, methodical, creative in his thinking. Knew how to play with his work – and win.

James gazed around the room to catch the eye of those he loved. Only Olivia was missing. He had the greatest admiration for Marguerite. In bed he teased her as, 'My sexual reprobate, my feminist goddess of the land of erotica.' Sex with her was thrilling and imaginative, but never more so as when they were joined by Olivia or September and Angelica. These people genuinely loved each other unconditionally. For years James and his sisters had made love to each other. Naked, they would lie down together, kissing and fondling each other's young flesh. It was affection, passion for a loved one of the highest order, but they never had intercourse. That seemed an unnatural act to them whereas kissing and amorousness for each other's flesh, heart and soul were not.

He studied Marguerite. Never had he seen her so animated, so beautiful. Her intelligence was shining like a star this evening. She looked every inch the special lady that she was but there was a new softness to her. She was in love with Neville as she had never been in love with James. Love between them had petered out years before though the sex had lingered on. No longer. Looking at her now he saw that even the sex had run its course.

James's eyes now sought out Harry. He liked Harry Graves-Jones but was concerned to find him in charge of the investigation. If anyone were to find Olivia it would be this man. James wondered, as he had a hundred times since Olivia had run away, if she was still alive. The nightmare to end all nightmares for James would be her death. In the last few days he had come to terms with never seeing her again. So long as she was alive and making a new life for herself somewhere, anywhere, that would have to be enough for him.

He rose from his chair and, taking the cognac bottle from the table, walked among his friends, serving them generously. Marguerite watched him. He had been so very good to her. For a few months they had loved each other deeply and thought they could make it work forever. She knew now they would always be friends. Her ties to the Buchanans and Olivia were indissoluble. She placed an arm around Neville. He understood the erotic attachment the group felt for one another. Not only had he accepted it but appreciated the freedom of their sexual lives and joined them. The group embodied love and devotion on a grand scale, ignoring all social and sexual rules. They might try to find another way to live but he had no doubt they could never fully abandon this way of life, their ideals. They had lived with each other too long to be parted. That was why Olivia's disappearance, vanishing as if in mid-air from their lives, was such a trauma to them all.

Marguerite turned to Harry and said, 'In my truth game there are no restrictions on what one can ask, but the answer must always be the truth. Are you ready, Harry?'

'Shall I kick off?' enquired Joe.

'Excuse me, but may I see you alone for a moment, sir?' Jenny intervened.

Once alone in the kitchen with Harry she came straight to the point. 'I'm confused, sir. This is highly unorthodox. I don't know what I'm supposed to do when these people are obviously obstructing justice.'

'You don't like them, do you?'

'No, I certainly don't!'

'Then, for Christ's sake, stop whinging and go for them! That's what I intend to do, and *I* like them,' retorted Harry.

'I'm sorry, sir, I should have worked that out for myself.'

Harry started for the door to the dining-room. 'Yes, you should have.'

Chapter 14

Ever since the tabloids had announced that Olivia had murdered the prince and vanished without trace, Marguerite had been trying to put the pieces of the mystery together. Since the detectives had arrived in Sefton Under Edge and interviewed everyone in the village and the Park, she had not been able to put Olivia out of her mind. She had taken notes, gone over what evidence she could gather, and felt that if she could reach a solution she might help allay the anxiety that she and Olivia's closest friends were experiencing. The guilt each of them felt for not having the chance to help her in this, the worst time of her life, weighed heavily on them all. The people closest to Olivia were now in her drawing-room and as Marguerite scanned it she knew that she had done the right thing by instigating this evening.

The detectives returned and took their seats. Marguerite began, 'Detective Constable Sixsmith, you had a question?'

'Many questions, Miss Chen. But let me begin by asking you if you aided Lady Olivia's escape from justice?'

'No, I did not,' she replied.

Joe continued around the room with the same question to every person there except Jenny and Harry. Every answer was the same as Marguerite's.

'I have a question,' James put in. 'Harry, how can you be so sure Olivia was responsible for the prince's death? How can you possibly know what happened that evening? Surely all you really know is that she was seen running away from the house, and some prurient details about the sexual games they enjoyed playing together. Olivia has become fodder for the gutter press, is being tried by them. They're no better than a kangaroo court.'

Harry recognised the passion in his voice. He was reminded that James, September, Angelica, Marguerite, Miss Plumm, these people who had known Olivia for most of her life, had loved her beyond reason because she lived at the very top of her life, as if every day might be her last. She had beauty and grace, a love of life, a generous, one might even say, opulent heart. She had passion and a love for the erotic that knew no bounds. She dazzled her lovers and her friends with her boundless energy and ability to live high, wide and handsome. How many times had they also seen the dark side of her and never acknowledged it as such?

'I have to agree with you, James, about the press. Marguerite, I am indebted to you for bringing us all together in this way. But if we do manage to put the pieces together, are you all sure you will like the picture we might make?'

'We must know the truth. Whatever it is, we'll have to accept it but I'm sure that not one of us in this room will abandon her. We will remain loyal to Olivia. We are, after all, the closest thing to a real family that she has,' September told him.

'Will you all give your word that you will not aid and abet her? I don't think so,' said Jenny bitterly.

The group remained silent. Harry could not be angry with Jenny. It was a good question though asked too soon. 'That's an interesting point. I would like you all to consider it but not to answer just yet. Take your time,' he instructed them.

Jenny felt angry and frustrated when Harry gave the group time to work out their answers. The frustration lingered on but her anger with Harry was short-lived. The moment she'd opened her mouth she had realised she was jumping too far ahead of events but been unable to stop. She'd wanted to catch them off guard, point up their questionable morals. She was a good enough detective to see that they were vulnerable and took some delight in seeing the group squirm now. At least she had made them uncomfortable, having to work out how to be loyal and an informer at the same time.

Marguerite took the floor again when she proposed, 'Let's begin at the beginning, the night of the so-called murder.'

'Not "so-called", just plain murder, Miss Chen,' Jenny insisted.

'Then why don't you tell me what you saw when you arrived at the scene of the crime that night?' asked Marguerite.

Jenny flushed pink and remained silent.

'Oh, I see, you did not visit the crime scene that

evening,' deduced Marguerite.

'Talk about kangaroo courts! Do sit down, Marguerite,' said Neville. 'Were you and Sixsmith there, Harry? And is it necessary for us to hear what happened that evening?'

'Yes. Sixsmith and I were there less than an hour after the crime had been committed. And, yes, I think you should all know the truth about that evening, not what the tabloids are telling you, nor what you want to believe because you are all intimately involved with Olivia.

'Marguerite, the two girls working in the kitchen . . . may I suggest you send them home. I want nothing said in this room overheard and becoming village gossip. We have kept the journalists at bay so far and I hope, for your sake, I can continue to lay other trails for them to follow and leave you all in peace. The last thing we need is a leak from this village.'

'I see your point,' said Marguerite, leaving the room.

While she was gone the men lit cigars and the women talked among themselves. Banal, stultifyingly boring chat about the village fête that not one of them would ever indulge in under other circumstances. The relief on their faces when Marguerite returned was obvious.

'They're gone, happy as sandboys to be off without doing all the chores.'

Harry began, 'We will start with the evening of the murder. The first thing I heard was that a woman was being chased through the streets of Mayfair by a man claiming to be the murder victim's brother. He identified the woman as Lady Olivia Cinders and kept shouting her name and that she had murdered his brother. A neighbour saw Olivia as she shot out of the front door of the prince's house. The neighbour identified the woman on the run as Lady Olivia. Several people joined in the chase but lost her.

'Once I'd had a call to go to the scene of the murder and had heard about the chase, I ordered every man available to comb the streets. If she were still on foot, she could not escape the ring we had around her, or so I believed. Sullivan was not at the scene of the crime because she was organising the hunt. We had Lady Olivia trapped, we thought.'

'She must have been frightened out of her wits,' said Angelica.

'Or drugged out of her head *and* frightened out of her wits, otherwise she would never have run,' offered September.

'That's an assumption and we're dealing with fact and truth here tonight,' corrected Joe Sixsmith.

'I find this all very painful. It's so out of character for Olivia to lose control of her life by committing such a deed and running away. It had to be a moment of insanity,' observed Miss Plumm.

'But is it true that her behaviour that evening *was* out of character? What if it were not? What if she had exercised the dark side of her nature before, possibly not in murder but in other more subtle ways which she took great pains to cover up so as not to shock you? You were after all family of a sort and one does not want to alienate those one loves or lose those who love you beyond reason. Just a hint of her naughtiness to make you all aware what she was capable of and because she was not one to hide? Up front honesty was all part of her charm. She was incredibly honest with you all and with herself, gave you hints as to who she was and what she was capable of. But you forgave her everything and never questioned that streak of blackness she carried in her soul.'

The silence in the room was deafening. It fell to Jenny to break it. Her superior was going hard on the group. She realised Harry intended the people in this room to validate his theory.

'You wanted this truth game so let's play it out. Is the Chief Inspector correct? Put any feelings of guilt aside and answer truthfully,' Jenny told them.

Marguerite spoke up. 'I think that is a pretty good assessment. I'll answer for all of us unless anyone thinks it incorrect. If so, speak up.'

No one said a word. 'Well, at last we all accept that Lady Olivia was capable of murder,' said Harry, looking at September who had become anxious and pale and was twisting a handkerchief in her hands.

'I have a question,' said Neville. 'Did you find any tangible evidence at the scene of the crime that Olivia had in fact been there? I know she was seen running from the house but that doesn't put her in the prince's bedroom?'

'These are the facts. By the time Sixsmith and I arrived at the house, there were dozens of uniforms and plain clothes around it seeing that nothing was disturbed. The prince's servants were assembled in the entrance hall, hysterical with grief. His brother was in the library on the telephone to the family. He put the phone down as soon as he saw us and made outrageous demands about our turning Lady Olivia over to him so she could be tried for murder in his country's courts.

'I walked from the library, telling him to calm down. I said I would return to talk with him after I had viewed the bedroom and his brother's body. He was still ranting and raving against Lady Olivia in French, English and Arabic as I closed the library door. He called her a whore, a killer, claimed she was common as dirt and that she had cast a spell on his brother. He was crazed with grief. The house was very beautiful, serenely so, in marked contrast to the ugliness of murder and mayhem upstairs.

'Two policemen were guarding the door to the bedroom. The officers stepped aside. On entering the room, which comprised the entire second floor, I was overwhelmed by an acrid scent masked by perfume. Patchouli. It was sickeningly sweet. It was an eerie scene, that magnificent room, and the gory, pitiful spectacle of a man with a peach-coloured chiffon scarf trailing from his mouth, tied to the headboard of his bed by wrists that had been slashed. Blood had pooled on the bed to either side of him.'

'The papers said a sex game gone wrong?' said Miss Plumm.

'The papers were wrong. I was wrong. My first impression was that this had been an accidental death when a sex game had gone wrong. Snuff sex! Sex to the death, that was what Lady Olivia wanted us to believe. But it was premeditated murder. She planned it brilliantly and her escape was even more clever and original.

She tossed out one red herring after another for us to follow while she got away.'

'Those are assumptions, not facts,' put in Marguerite who looked as shocked as the rest of the group.

'I'm afraid not. Those are facts based on evidence I was unable to pull together until this afternoon. Please believe me when I tell you I would rather it had been accidental death. I had become smitten with Lady Olivia, learned to admire her as you do. But having come to Sefton Under Edge and learned all about her from the interviews we conducted here, a picture emerged that I had not expected. I believe she might never have committed murder if she had broken up with the prince. But I digress. Back to the night of the murder and the bedroom. Sixsmith, you take it from here: forensics report.'

Joe Sixsmith paced the floor as he spoke. 'Lady Olivia and the prince had had intercourse several times during the afternoon and evening. There was evidence to show the prince had been tied up a while before his wrists were slashed. He was high as a kite on cocaine and alcohol.

'We know the time Lady Olivia was discovered by the prince's brother and fled the house. An autopsy showed the prince was already dead then. Which means that the time between Lady Olivia's inflicting those wounds on him and fleeing the house was considerable. We know that she slit his wrists because she left the knife she'd used on the bed. It had no fingerprints on it but hers.

'She stuffed her scarf in his mouth, sat there and watched him die. Now why would she take pleasure in watching his life ebb away? Did she reap a sexual thrill from it? Did he, expecting Lady Olivia to save him in the nick of time? Was she as drugged as he was? I doubt that somehow. Lady Olivia gave up the idyllic life she had going for her, for the pleasure of seeing him die. It took hours for his life to ebb away. She could have left before the end came but she didn't. She had to see him dead. What possessed her to kill him? If there were mitigating circumstances, we should know about them. That might be to her advantage.'

Harry walked around the room, examining the faces of those assembled. His heart went out to September. He was causing her so much pain that when their eyes met she had to look away. Angelica was white with distress. James had his head bowed and the palms of his hands covering his face. Marguerite, chin high, was given away by the deadness in her eyes, the tears she was struggling to hold back.

'How were you able to deduce it was a premeditated killing, Harry?' she asked.

'I had not the slightest suspicion that it had been a premeditated act of violence until I interviewed her friends in this place she loved so much. I came to know her through the people who loved her and would remain loyal to her, no matter what. Finally I could step into her skin and work out why she never went to them for help. I had come to believe that every one of you who told me that you had not seen or heard from her was telling the truth. The question then arose: why wouldn't Lady Olivia go to her friends for help?'

Marguerite jumped up from her chair. 'Because she didn't need any! She had it all worked out: the killing, the sex game gone wrong, the escape!'

'Very good, Marguerite.'

'But something unexpected happened. The prince's brother walked in on the scene. She'd never expected to be caught in the house. But it was only a small hitch in her plans. She was so organised she had only to get out of Mayfair as quickly as possible,' Marguerite deduced.

'That seems to me to be right,' said Jenny, grudgingly.

'James, why would Lady Olivia go to such lengths to kill the prince? What would have driven her to murder him in such a bizarre fashion and enjoy his pain and suffering? She had to know that she would be the obvious suspect, that she would have to go on the run for the remainder of her life, change her identity, if she hoped to escape being convicted?' asked Harry.

'I can't answer that, I simply don't know. She had a love-hate relationship with the prince. He was possessive and jealous and pushed his drugging and sexual proclivities over the edge of sanity or pleasure. He dragged Olivia into that world too and brought out in her passions she could not resist exploiting to the point of no return. I don't just mean sexually. He had a power over her that she would both enjoy and resist. There was nothing she wouldn't do to bring him pleasure. But he was the same with her,' said James.

'He could make her do anything he wanted. Is it possible she obeyed one order too many and could not live with herself for having done so? Or that he had humiliated her once too often? He never did that to her in public, dared not. He knew she would walk away from him if he did. She often told him, as she told us, that she would do just that when their affair had run its course.

Olivia believed that she had control and yet more than a few times she tried to leave him but had not the will to follow through. It was just not possible. She was angry with herself and him. I think she came to understand that he would keep her for himself no matter what she wanted,' said Angelica.

'He was a known sexual thrill-seeker, a sometime sadist. Something Olivia was not. He was always trying to corrupt her that little bit more,' Marguerite declared.

'He understood but could never accept that love, passion, forthrightness, adventure, governed Olivia's life. In a strange way he loved and hated her for having those qualities. Every one of her friends believed that when she was through playing with her wild prince she would leave him. She had us all convinced she could. Now this! Quite obviously she came to understand she was his prisoner and he would never let her go. The drugs and the bizarre sex life they led altered her. She became two people: the Olivia we all loved and adored and the prince's Olivia. He liked her dark soul, exploited it, taught her to embrace it. She used to say teasingly, "Embrace me, my dark mysterious soul," ' said Miss Plumm.

'No wonder you all feel so guilty. You let her run headlong into this situation and now you've lost her forever and a man has been brutally murdered,' Jenny observed bitterly.

'Sullivan!' There was reproach in Harry's voice.

'Yes, sir,' she answered, nearly jumping to attention.

There was a tense moment in the room until he broke the silence, calmly suggesting, 'Let's review what we have on the abandoned car, which in fact is what first brought us to Sefton Under Edge. Sullivan, you start.'

'We know about the abandoned car,' said Marguerite.

'Do we? That's how good detecting goes. Review the facts, again and again, until you have understood them and they provide a solution to your particular question. Proceed, Sullivan.'

September gazed into Harry's eyes, transfixed by admiration for him. He never ceased to surprise her with that outer softness over a hard core. This was the man with whom she had fallen in love at first sight. She didn't want to believe what he was saying: that Olivia had planned and plotted to kill the prince and to run away from them all to live a new life. Tears trickled from her eyes. Olivia had broken her heart. September knew Olivia loved her and it had not been deliberate, it was simply a sad by-product of Olivia's having to rid herself of the prince once and for all.

Harry saw the distress in September's face, the tears staining her cheeks. He went to her and sat on the arm of her chair to be close to her. She would understand that it was impossible for him to do more for her at that moment.

'Sullivan?' he pressed.

'Lady Olivia, having fled the prince's house and eluded the hunt for her, appeared at the Wasboroughs'. She borrowed Mrs Wasborough's car and ten thousand pounds, gave no excuse for her actions and drove out of London. She told her friend that she would see that her car was returned. Lady Olivia drove the car to Sefton Under Edge and abandoned it, continuing her escape on foot or by plane from here with the help of friends.'

'Wrong,' said Marguerite.

'Why?' asked Harry.

'Ten thousand pounds? How far would that get Olivia? No. She would have gone to where she had stashed several hundred thousand at least, picked it up, then flown herself out of England. That is if, and it is a big if, she had planned this murder.'

'Very good, Marguerite!' said an impressed Harry.

'Then who drove the car to Sefton Under Edge? Do you mean she was never even here that night? How can you be sure? She might have hidden the money in the woods, driven here to get it, and then had a driver to take her to her next destination,' said Jenny.

Silence hung like smoke over the room. Olivia's friends were dazed by what was being said. It was Joe Sixsmith who spoke up. 'Two people drove the car here, that was why both doors were left open?'

'Wrong!' said Marguerite most emphatically.

She looked over at Harry. Her mind was ticking like a time bomb. She was mentally putting the pieces together and the picture was strong and clear as nothing about Olivia's disappearance had been until now.

Jenny Sullivan was irritated by every word Marguerite said. She tried to take over once more. 'Why are you so sure that's wrong?'

'Both car doors were open – that was to make us think two people had been in the car. The lights left on? An indication of timing to hoodwink the police. The keys in the ignition to imply a hurried departure. A thumb and forefinger print left deliberately so as to identify Olivia as having been in the car. The car parked across the road to cause an obstruction. Another puzzle for the police. There was a twofold purpose to that: had she come here to seek help in the village or the Park? The abandoned car was just a red herring for New Scotland Yard to waste their time on. No, Olivia never came to Sefton Under Edge. She was following her original plan,' deduced Marguerite as she walked to the drinks table and poured herself another calvados.

'You will never find her, Harry,' said James, looking decidedly anxious.

Harry felt James's pain. Time would heal that and out of kindness the detective kept quiet. He did not tell James that he would pursue Lady Olivia Cinders until he had arrested her or had proof of her death, no matter how many years it took. He and the Yard would never close the file on her.

Chapter 15

Marguerite asked Neville to bring in two bottles of champagne and the ice bucket. She went to sit next to James. 'Are you bearing up?' she asked.

'Yes, just about,' he told her. She stroked his cheek.

'That's just about how we're all taking this, James,' said Angelica, who went to him, sat on his lap, and leaned against his chest.

Harry was mesmerised by the love and affection, the degree of genuine caring, this group of people showed towards one another without any shame. Marguerite, September, Angelica and James were open in the way they caressed, kissed and spoke to each other. It was a kind of intimacy rarely achieved. They gave each other everything and achieved something so special that Harry yearned to be part of it. He thought of Lady Olivia, and how she would never have this special something from them again. He understood, as they did, as surely Olivia must, the terrible price she had paid for her freedom.

Out of the corner of his eye, he caught a glimpse of Jenny Sullivan, stunned to silence by the behaviour of James, Angelica and Marguerite. He could see the shock in her face as she watched them together. She saw something she could never have because she simply did not understand it, and he felt pity for her.

Neville returned and opened the champagne, Marguerite filled glasses. And then Harry said, 'Marguerite, I would not be best pleased to see you go into print with a book on the disappearance of Lady Olivia Cinders.'

'You have my word I will never write about this. There will be plenty of other people fascinated by Olivia's disappearance who will try and write it for some fast money. But exploit her misery? I would never do that.'

'So let's recap,' said Harry as he drew up a chair close to Miss Plumm's.

'We now believe that the murder of the prince by Lady Olivia was premeditated. That she has snookered New Scotland Yard and this investigation by planting false clues to keep the Yard busy while she makes a clean getaway,' said Joe Sixsmith.

'A little bald and not very elegantly worded but basically correct,' agreed Harry.

'This new theory seems the more probable of any so far. But it does pose new questions. "Follow the money and you'll find your criminal," some famous detective once said. I forgot which one but it seems like sound advice,' said Marguerite.

'You seem to be very good at this, Marguerite. Possibly too good,' commented James.

'Now what does that mean?' she asked.

'Should we, Olivia's friends, go any further in helping to find her? Is that what she would want? We have to ask ourselves that question.'

Miss Plumm began to laugh and all attention was now focused on her. When she had herself under control, she said, 'My dear James, Olivia has set us all up in a game where she is holding the key cards. If she were here right now she'd be laughing and teasing us because of it. Yes, indeed, she would want us to play her game, even if she is playing *in absentia*.'

'Well, if that's what she expects then we shan't deny her a last game with us,' he said.

Marguerite too began to laugh. 'A deadly game, and that's not just a pun. Now that we have worked it out, I can see that the path she chose to take was the only one open to her. It was a matter of survival; one of them had to die to be free from the other. It was merely a question of who would get there first. Olivia's will to live was stronger than her passionate and sick relationship with the prince. He intended to keep her locked away in one of his palaces, as a sexual toy for himself and his friends. And she, having realised that was his object, plotted and planned her revenge and escape.'

Jenny Sullivan was lost with not the least idea of what Marguerite was implying. Joe Sixsmith did not have that problem, he was very much tuned in to what she was saying.

'Now we have a motive for the murder,' he announced.

'Miss Chen, those are mere assumptions on your part. You have created a motive,' Jenny was quick to declare.

'They are *not* assumptions, Detective Constable Sullivan. They're fact. Olivia told us of the depraved acts the prince demanded of her, and that she had willingly acceded. At first. Later she told us that he intended to

225

kidnap her and keep her as a sex slave, and assured us that would never happen. That if it were to come to that it would be Olivia who would survive,' said Angelica.

'So now we have the motive,' agreed James.

'Marguerite, did you at any time think she meant to kill the prince?' asked Harry.

'Never!'

'Then how do you account for his death?' asked Jenny.

'Because Olivia wanted to live, I've already told you, Detective Constable Sullivan.'

'Then you believe as she did, that he would have killed her before letting her go?' verified Jenny.

'Does any of this really matter?' Neville put in.

'Only in as much as it goes towards motive. But let's move on. Olivia found the right moment to destroy her lover. He went along with the bondage, being made love to by her, forced to keep silent. We will never know until we hear it from Olivia's own lips what happened next. Did he still believe it was part of their sexual game when she slit his wrists? Had they planned that together? Had he done it in search of a new sexual high? If he had been willingly participating in this act, he made the fatal mistake of believing she would save him. I believe she had been planning to murder him for some time and this opportunity arose. It was perfect. Afterwards she sat on the bed with him and watched him slowly die.'

'She was watching the darkness of her soul ooze away with every drop of his blood,' put in Miss Plumm. 'I know Olivia – she was purging herself of the darkness that had taken over her life. Wherever she is, whatever she is doing now, she will be free and enjoying life. She will miss us as we will miss her but she will have worked out that it is better for her to be free and the wondrous person she can be than dead and gone forever like her dark prince.'

'Miss Plumm, I believe you to be right. But how was she so sure that New Scotland Yard would not find her and bring her to justice?' asked Harry.

'Olivia would have refused even to countenance such a possibility. She will have planned her new life carefully, accepting she'll be hunted always but never captured,' answered Miss Plumm.

'The brother's arrival was unexpected bad luck, while finding the Wasboroughs at home was a stroke of good fortune. Borrowing Caroline Wasborough's car was how she was able to get out of Mayfair. But where did she go then? Who drove the car to Sefton Under Edge?' asked Harry.

'That was where she was really clever,' Marguerite maintained. 'Olivia knew that she was going to kill the prince that day. She would have known that the Wasboroughs weren't going out that night – she was always talking to Caroline. The ten thousand pounds was nothing to Olivia, she probably took it to make herself look desperate. Remember, everything was done to make the killing look like a sexual prank gone wrong.

'So, she's got the car and some money and has to get the car to Sefton Under Edge and create a mystery around it. But most of all she has to get out of England as fast as possible, within an hour of the murder. She could only do that one way: with the assistance of a villain who was on stand-by all along. Olivia would have

227

paid them a huge sum, fifty or a hundred thousand pounds in non-traceable notes. Enough to keep them silent forever.'

'How would she know such a person?' asked Jenny.

'I don't know. But Olivia always managed to get anything she needed because she knew that money talks,' said Marguerite.

'So Olivia had this driver on stand-by during the night in question? It sounds a bit far-fetched,' said James.

Marguerite slapped her hand down on the table. 'Precisely. And that was why it would work. It would have been some place central, all she had to do was drive to it and step out of the car for a minute to signal the person in question. It would have been somewhere central, packed with people. A McDonald's, Burger King, fish-and-chip shop . . . somewhere she would never normally be seen dead in. The man is there waiting, joins her and gets instructions as to exactly how she wants the car dealt with. He drives her to her destination, and Olivia pays him off. Not long after she has been chased through the streets of Mayfair, she's out of London and on her way into exile.'

'And you said you weren't going to write a novel about the disappearance of Lady Olivia!' Jenny Sullivan laughed sarcastically.

Harry stood up and was about to dress Jenny down for her rudeness but was stopped by Marguerite who held up her hand, palm out towards him, as a signal for him to let her speak.

'You know, Detective Constable Sullivan, I don't understand what your problem is but clearly you have one with being here in my house and playing this truth game. You think me and my friends frivolous, have been rude to us on more than one occasion, patently disapprove of this evening and what is being accomplished, and have made it more than obvious that you are hell-bent on wielding your authority as a policewoman.

'None of that is very smart. You're so adversarial most of the time, and jealous, and just plain bigoted against Olivia and her lifestyle, that you are missing the plain fact that we are helping you understand what actually happened. Why don't you cut out the attitude and try and get as much as you can out of this exercise?'

Jenny could hardly take her eyes off Marguerite. She detested this woman for her success and her posturing but everything Marguerite said was true. Jenny had no defence to offer.

'I think I owe you an apology, Miss Chen. May I take the floor and ask a question?'

'Well, that's what we're here for,' answered a still angry but gracious Marguerite.

'If your scenario is right, where did she get the money? We've had all her accounts frozen and investigated, and for months before the murder no large sums had been liquidated,' Jenny explained.

'Good question, Detective Constable Sullivan. But Olivia was smart about money, knew very well how costly a lifestyle she enjoyed. And the prince spoiled her rotten. She would have worked out that she might never be able to touch her money if she vanished in such circumstances. My guess is that she had other funds, banked secretly. I believe she got millions from the prince. Ten, or twenty million dollars was pin money to him. Who's to say? Maybe fifty or a hundred million. That would be enough to bankroll her escape?

'If she didn't get the money from the prince then she might have got it from one of her other admirers, a secret one. He would have to be a powerful man, above investigation and able to protect her. Someone worth billions of dollars and a law unto himself. And certainly a man who disliked the prince. Would she have fled to such a person? I doubt it. If Olivia didn't trust us to help her then she would not trust anyone else. No. She picked up her fortune, paid off her villain, and having bought a small jet aircraft, loaded the money aboard and flew away from England while you, Harry, were still examining the scene of the crime.'

'I don't mean to be rude, Miss Chen, but you're painting an imaginary picture and we need facts!' Jenny objected.

'Well, I don't mean to be rude either but that's *your* problem. You haven't crawled into Olivia's skin and thought as she thought, used your imagination, followed your hunches. Harry has, and so has DC Sixsmith. I gave you a scenario. Why not do some work on it, get some more clues? Follow the money, that's where you'll find Olivia,' Marguerite declared.

'Yes, you're very good at this. You have at least given us some idea of how she might have eluded us,' Harry confirmed.

Turning to face Jenny, he told her, 'Go down to the office and get the following things under way: bank statements going back one year. Find out from the prince's secretary if the prince made any large sums of money over to Lady Olivia. They would be cash transactions. Get the boys down at the Yard to check out all the small jet planes sold in the last year and find out to whom. Then return here with your notes about the flights that were made on the night of the murder.'

After Jenny had left, Miss Plumm suggested coffee might be in order and September offered to make it. Marguerite's head was still spinning with many possible explanations for what had happened to Olivia. She felt suddenly queasy. Aloud she said, 'What if she is dead? If she was capable of deliberately killing the prince then it has to be a possibility that she has taken her own life or is prepared to do so if she has to. Harry, you'll never capture her alive. Let her go. She's better free than dead.'

'I doubt that that is even a remote possibility. What we are all failing to acknowledge is that she *did* get clean away and by now is already installed in her new life. She's no more behaving as a hunted woman than I am,' argued Miss Plumm.

The relief on everyone's face at this argument was obvious. Even Harry and Joe felt relieved to hear that their murderer was not the type to kill herself. Joe was by now as caught up in the mystery and charm of Lady Olivia and as determined to bring her to justice as Harry. It was he who asked the group, 'So where are we now?'

'Just where she wants us to be. Still in the dark. I wonder when she expected us to come to our senses and realise she's been sending us on false trails right from the start? Not yet, I wager,' observed Harry.

Neville spoke up. 'Marguerite's quite right, you must follow the money.'

'First you have to find it,' offered Angelica.

'Good point. Has anyone any ideas where she might have stashed that amount of cash?' asked Marguerite.

September returned to the drawing-room with a tray laden with coffee cups and saucers and a silver service. She placed it in front of Miss Plumm and asked her to serve. Angelica and Marguerite declared themselves famished and went to the kitchen to make sandwiches. James looked troubled and got to his feet.

'Don't you think we're behaving like turncoats?' he asked.

'No, James. We're trying to solve the mystery of what happened to Olivia. Even if it helps the police, it will get them nowhere. Olivia means never to be found. The police can look for her for an eternity, they'll never find her. That's the truth and we all know it,' said September.

'Do we really believe that?'

'Yes,' they all said together.

There was not a person in that room who believed Olivia would ever be captured. Harry tried to shake off the feeling; it was his job to find her and bring her to trial, after all. Every loose end had to be tied up before he and his team left Sefton Under Edge. Olivia had thrown them more red herrings than was imaginable. But, he had to ask himself, might there have been one that had not been just another ruse, some small mistake that would give him a clue as to how she had managed to slip his net at every turn?

Marguerite returned with a platter heaped with ham

and cheese sandwiches. Suddenly everyone felt hungry. They devoured their sandwiches and drank their coffee. It was during that midnight feast that Harry came to realise how badly the disappearance of Lady Olivia Cinders had affected them all. He could now understand why Marguerite had to lay her ghost before any of them could proceed with a life without her.

Suddenly Marguerite put down her sandwich and gazed at him. 'What is it, Harry? I know there's something on your mind.'

Everyone stopped eating and all eyes turned to him. 'One of Lady Olivia's red herrings turns out to be a possible clue,' he announced.

Before he could continue, Marguerite interrupted, 'The so-called hunter in Jethroe's cap and jacket!'

'He was the villain she hired to drive the car and lay the Sefton Under Edge trap for us all to get caught up in. She bought the jacket and cap and dogs that looked as close to Jethroe's as possible – just to cover her tracks in case anyone saw him. And indeed someone did: the postman. Joe, first thing in the morning find that postman and have him go through the mug shots of known villains who might fit the description. Lady Olivia had everything worked out to the last detail.'

'So would you, Harry, if your life depended on it,' said September.

Marguerite looked at Harry. She really liked him, but he was Olivia's enemy. If anyone could find her it would be Harry. She could see that and also that it would never happen. She didn't feel sorry for him, he was not a man one pitied. Her thoughts switched to Olivia. Was she happy? Yes, of course she was. And no doubt already steeped in her new life. Did she have a lover yet? Was she living in a city or a remote part of the world where she would be safe? Was she still blonde and ravishingly beautiful or had she dyed her hair black and bought herself a new face? Marguerite could not believe she would destroy her looks. If she had done that then she might as well have killed herself. Wherever she was, whatever she was doing, she would always be the most ravishing English beauty, bursting with life and love.

Marguerite sighed heavily and looked away from Harry. He went to her and asked if something was wrong. 'No,' she replied. But he didn't believe her.

'When are you leaving, Harry?' asked Miss Plumm.

'In the morning.'

'Then you go away empty-handed?'

Harry thought that this was as good a time as any to let the secret become public knowledge. He looked across the room at September. She smiled at him and he felt her love and passion for him. He almost faltered then turned back to Miss Plumm. After raising her hand and kissing it, he announced, 'Not quite empty-handed, September is coming with me.'

Chapter 16

For Harry, one of the more unpleasant aspects of the Lady Olivia Cinders case was having to deal with the prince's brother and family who were running their own investigation. A team of the best private detectives were working round the clock and all over the world. They not only wanted the murderer of the prince, they wanted slowly and painfully to murder the murderer.

That was, of course, not possible so far as England and the Home Office were concerned. Harry had been fearful that they might find Olivia but after that evening at Marguerite's, he was certain it would never happen. If Lady Olivia were playing New Scotland Yard for fools, then she was making even greater ones out of the prince's family.

Jenny traced the prince's brother who was sailing the Côte d'Azure on his ocean-going yacht. Harry had made an appointment to meet the prince the following day at the marina in Nice. But for the moment, driving into London with September at his side, he could think of nothing but the woman he loved.

'I'm not a wealthy man, September,' he told her after

they had been driving in silence for some time.

'You're the richest man I know. You've got me,' was her reply as she snuggled up closer.

'You're very sure about us, aren't you?'

'And you aren't?' she enquired.

'You know better than that!'

'Then why are we having this conversation?'

'Because I've never been in love like this before. Because I'm driving back into the city a different man: one committed to loving you. Because I feel the excitement of sharing my life with another human being and being loved on such a grand scale.'

Harry pulled the car over to the soft shoulder and turned off the motor. He pulled her into his arms and they kissed passionately. Then Harry caressed September's hair and grazed her cheek with the back of his hand. 'It's going to seem like an eternity before we get home,' he told her.

At last he left the car in the courtyard of Albany and, arm in arm, they walked up the stairs to his set of rooms. He opened the door and carried September over the threshold. She was charmed by the old-fashioned rooms and commented, 'Sherlock Holmes could have lived here.'

'He does, only he's changed his name to Harry Graves-Jones. How does September Graves-Jones sound to you?' he asked.

'Music to my ears,' she told him, and jumped into his arms. He caught her and they laughed as he carried her to the bedroom.

September closed her eyes and bit the back of her

hand as copious and strong orgasms took her over and transported her into an erotic nirvana. There was something about Harry's body scent, the texture of his skin, the way he was formed . . . he was incredibly sexy to her. She was never happier than when she was in the throes of sex, but this was that and more. She gave in to her orgasms, one following another quite quickly, and Harry bathed himself in them and adored her even more for her lustfulness. His sexuality, his love for her, was overwhelming.

September felt she need never hold back sexually from Harry. He wanted everything erotic to be played out in their lives. They would give each other everything and dwell in a private world of all things lustful that gave them pleasure.

Long after September fell asleep in his arms, Harry lay awake thinking about Olivia and how he must never let her come between his love and himself.

Over breakfast, buttered toast with lashings of Cooper's marmalade and coffee in bed, he said, 'I think it would be a good idea not to bring home my work, so to speak.'

'So that Olivia will not come between us? I think that's a very good idea. We have a life of our own to build.'

'You are so special, my love. Beautiful, clever, creative, sensitive and understanding. You make my life rich and full where previously it was empty. Thank you,' he told her.

They woke early because September wanted to show him her London studio. It was amazing, once the entire floor, the loft of a great house with a perfect north light flowing through half a dozen arched windows. And, unbelievably, it was a corner site in Knightsbridge with a view of the park.

'It's fantastic. However did you find it?' he asked.

'The family owns the building,' she answered.

Harry laughed. He felt as if he belonged in the studio in the same way he felt at home in Sefton Park.

'We're one of those families that are property rich and always cash poor. Do you mind?' she asked teasingly because she knew he didn't.

Harry took the afternoon flight to Nice and a taxi from the airport to the marina where he was met by four of the crew of the *Gloriana*, the dead prince's yacht. He was taken from there by motor launch directly to the yacht anchored a mile off the coast.

Harry's first impression was of the vessel's size and beauty. Once on board he realised that Olivia had had a hand in the design of the interior. This was no gin palace awash with marble and gilt. It was like the prince's bedroom or Olivia's own rooms at Albany: grand yet impressively simple.

Harry was shown into the library where he was offered tea and small bite-sized sandwiches of smoked salmon. When, after an hour, he was still waiting to see the prince's brother, he began to seethe with irritation. After two hours he rang the service bell and asked to be taken ashore. It was half an hour after that that the prince's brother appeared. There was no apology.

'Detective Chief Inspector Graves-Jones, have you any positive news for me? That, for instance, you have captured my brother's murderer.'

'No, sir, I'm not able to tell you that.'

'Then why are you here?'

'Because I have reason to believe that Lady Olivia Cinders had received a substantial sum of money some time before she murdered your brother. I am trying to trace that money, who gave it to her and what she did with it.'

'A bit slow, weren't you? Follow the money and you will always find your villain. We've been on that for weeks.'

'And?' asked Harry.

'And, nothing,' answered the prince bitterly.

'How much did your brother give her?' probed Harry.

The prince paced the room, picked up the telephone and ordered coffee. Then, turning back to Harry, he said, 'Olivia has been devilishly clever. My brother bought her for eighty million dollars. She refused to become his forever until that sum was deposited in a Swiss account. She toyed with him for almost eight months after she received the money.

'The first thing I did after my brother was murdered was to go after that money. I knew where it was – or, rather, I thought I knew where it was. Olivia collected the money a week after it was deposited in the bank. She used to tease my brother that it was her insurance, her getaway fund, so he had better stay in love with her and in line. Don't waste your time speculating about that money. You have to find it before you can follow it and so far, just like Olivia, it has vanished without trace.'

The two men gazed at each other, equally determined

to find Olivia. For the first time, the prince realised that Harry Graves-Jones would never give up this hunt. They were comrades-in-arms who would become enemies once Olivia had been found. Harry Graves-Jones would never turn her over to the prince. His sense of justice, his Englishness, would never allow it. Harvard-educated and worldly, the prince loved the west but a passion for the power and the justice of Islam was bred into him.

'Is there anything else you can tell me?' asked Harry, mostly because he couldn't think of anything else to say. He had come to find out about the money and he had. There was little more to say or do.

He had ways and means of tracing large sums and would try them all. That was all he had to go on. Every lead to finding Olivia seemed always to come to a dead end. When the prince shook his head, Harry asked if he might be put ashore now.

'At once. I will walk you to the deck.'

He felt uneasy with the prince and could hardly wait to be out of his presence. There was something brutal about him despite the American accent and Armani clothes. He was darkly handsome with a short-cropped beard, should have made one feel he was one of a new generation who were done with acts of barbarism. But that was not the case.

'You will keep me informed?' asked the prince.

'Yes, and I hope you will do the same with me.'

As the two men walked through the various state rooms Harry saw several beautiful women, as stunning as catwalk mannequins, draped decoratively around the yacht. It was difficult to imagine Lady Olivia being one of them. It prompted him to ask his host, 'Did you know Olivia well?'

The prince said nothing for a minute and then, when they had reached the gangway that led to the motor launch, he answered Harry, 'Olivia enchanted me as she did my brother. I thought her dazzling, quintessentially English with all the right aristocratic connections. She was wildly free, gloriously beautiful, unimaginably sexy. My brother was besotted with her and I travelled with them frequently. We thought we had her bent to our will and that was our fatal mistake. Now she must die for what she has done to my family. Goodbye, Chief Inspector.'

Harry was halfway down the gangway when he turned and took the stairs two at a time, returning to the prince. 'One more thing – that tract of land in South Africa that your brother bought for her. Is there anything you can tell me about it?'

'That's the last place she would go. She knows it's the first place I would look. As I have done already. Olivia is not there.'

In the taxi on the way to the airport Harry kept thinking about the money and those sightings he had heard of from South Africa. Once more he climbed into Olivia's skin and tried to work out what she had done with the money and whether she was or was not in South Africa on her game reserve.

The papers were still full of reports about Olivia which Harry found irritating. He saw them in Nice airport and didn't bother to buy one. It was a two-hour wait before his flight was due to take off, and in those two hours an aspect of Olivia manifested itself that he had not considered before. Lady Olivia would not have committed that crime without understanding very well she would subsequently have to change her life and goals. That she would, in penance for her violent action, retreat from the shallow and sick world into which she had been dragged by the prince. No doubt she had retreated with her money to a place where she could make a difference without incurring any notoriety.

But was he right? So many times he'd thought he had fathomed Olivia and never received any proof that that was so. Restless, he called September. The message he found on her studio answer machine was, 'I'm on the way to the airport to meet your plane. I still love you.' Harry left the telephone booth smiling.

It was one of those glorious Indian summer days that can happen in September. Under a warm, clear, bright blue sky, the leaves on the trees were just beginning to turn coral and orange, yellow and rust. It was considered the society wedding of the year. And anyone who was anyone was going to be there. James, as head of the family, was giving the wedding as a gift to his sister. He was also giving September away. Neville was Harry's best man. Joe and Jenny were ushers, showing people to their pews. Marguerite and Angelica were in the wedding party as September's attendants. Miss Plumm was given a seat of honour close to the altar. The church looked splendid, dressed in white roses and Longee lilies. The men wore tails and old-fashioned fully-blown yellow roses in their lapels. The bride, dressed in her great-grandmother's white lace wedding dress, carried a waterfall of white moth orchids and was wearing the family's wedding and coronation diamond tiara.

There wasn't a room to be had in the area and the entrance to Sefton Park was patrolled by gatemen collecting invitations. The car park was outside the village and beautiful, elegantly dressed women and handsome men dressed in tails and carrying or wearing top hats, wandered through the village to the church. There were horse-drawn carriages for those who found the walk from the church to the reception in the Park a step too far. Everyone in the village was invited to attend the ceremony and the luncheon party as well as the wedding ball to be given that evening. Both *Hello* and *OK* as well as *Vogue* and *Tatler* were barred from the premises. Harry had organised tight but unobtrusive security.

The night before the wedding he spent at Miss Plumm's house. He had hardly any sleep. He had drunk and eaten too much at Sefton Park where the closest friends of the family had been invited to a sumptuous evening meal and a cello recital. Harry had never felt so loved or that he belonged anywhere so completely as he did the night before his wedding. At one point he and September sneaked off and made love in her bedroom then he went back to Miss Plumm's.

Many of the Buchanans' friends arrived in their bi-planes. Harry saw them on the grass like grand butterflies as he walked by. They were parked in a neat line, leaving the field free for others to land. Harry was not so much overwhelmed by the sheer scale of the wedding as entranced by the fun of it.

His colleagues were dazzled and quite obviously out of their depth until Harry told them, 'For God's sake, I just want you all to be yourselves and have a great time. I'm only going to do this once.'

As people walked to the church they were entertained by a string quartet playing near the duck pond. In the church, instead of organ music, there was a harpist and two flautists playing baroque music. The church bulged with guests and the service was short but touching, all the more romantic because someone had let white doves loose in the rafters: they seemed to coo and swoop at all the right moments.

'This is the most thrilling and happy day of my life,' Harry whispered in September's ear before he gave her the expected kiss at the end of the ceremony. Then they walked down the aisle and out into the sunlight.

There were streams of people walking down the road to Sefton Park and cheers for those who chose the open horse-drawn carriages. Miss Marble – who had of course made the wedding cake, a splendid five tiers decorated with blown sugar doves – rode by with her two helpers and the cake up the avenue of limes. It seemed to Harry that his wedding was like a cross between an upmarket fête and a grand party where everyone was bound to have the best time ever.

He and September rode from the church to the house in an open landau pulled by four white horses. With them were James and Angelica. They saw a host of round tables with slender vases containing white amaryllis. The sit-down dinner was for four hundred; the tables, draped in white silk organza and piped in white satin, ranged over the parkland with the house as a backdrop.

Everyone stood around drinking champagne and toasting the happy couple. Stewards arrived dressed in what had been the family livery and escorted people to their tables. The food was catered by Raymond Blanc and the service was lavish. A band was playing Rodgers and Hart, Cole Porter and George Gershwin while the guests ate their lunch.

Coffee was just being served and the after-dinner speeches were about to begin when the faint sound of an approaching bi-plane grew louder. Then, quite suddenly, it was swooping out of the sky over the heads of the guests before shooting straight up in the air and executing a perfect barrel roll. The pilot slowed the plane down and passed once more over the wedding party to toss hundreds of white roses from the cockpit. Then dipped the wings from side to side and was gone.

September, James and Angelica waved madly at the receding plane, until it was no more than a dot on the horizon. Harry was astounded, not so much by the daredevil display as by the fact that he had at last seen Lady Olivia Cinders's magnificent face, her blonde hair, and the smile that he would remember all his life.

•

Forbidden

Roberta Latow

Amy Ross, a celebrated art historian, has had many lovers in her lifetime. Again and again she has tasted the sweet ecstasy of sexual fulfilment and erotic depravity. Now, in her later years, she lives as a recluse, blissfully content in her own isolation, an enigma to her friends and admirers.

But Amy has suppressed the memory of her one secret obsession – her love affair with the artist Jarret Sparrow. Their relationship was beyond belief, her love for him dominated her entire life and took her to the furthest limits of carnal desire. Their feelings were too powerful to control – but their love for each other was ultimately forbidden.

Since their separation, Jarret and his manipulative Turkish friend Fee have seduced numerous women in pursuit of their ambition to conquer the art world. And now Jarret is about to re-enter Amy's life. For all those years, Amy had thought it was over. But is she prepared to rekindle the flames of her desire, and at what price . . . ?

'A wonderful storyteller. Her descriptive style is second to none . . . astonishing sexual encounters . . . exotic places, so real you can almost feel the hot sun on your back . . . heroines we all wish we could be' *Daily Express*

'Latow's writing is vibrant and vital. Her descriptions emanate a confidence and boldness that is typical of her characters' *Books* magazine

'It sets a hell of a standard' *The Sunday Times*

'Explicitly erotic . . . intelligently written' *Today*

0 7472 4911 3

HEADLINE

The Real Thing

Catherine Alliott

Everyone's got one – an old boyfriend they never fell out of love with, they simply parted because the time wasn't right. And for thirty-year-old Tessa, it's Patrick Cameron, the gorgeous, moody, rebellious boy she met at seventeen; the boy her vicar father thoroughly disapproved of; the boy who left her to go to Italy to paint.

And now he's back.

'You're in for a treat' *Express*

'Alliot's joie de vivre is irresistible' *Daily Mail*

'Compulsive and wildly romantic' *Bookseller*

'An addictive cocktail of wit, frivolity and madcap romance ... move over Jilly, your heir is apparent' *Time Out*

0 7472 5235 1

HEADLINE